About the Author

Kevin Bragg is a native of Detroit, who met a girl in Scotland, and now resides in the arboreal splendor of the Swedish hinterlands. He has been a great many things in his life; none of which relate to his academic pursuit of the Visigoths.

In Kevin's free time, he enjoys cooking, brewing beer, playing video games and standing in the garden pretending to be helpful.

Transilience is his debut novel.

TRANSILIENCE

TRANSILIENCE

KEVIN BRAGG

This edition first published in 2017

Unbound

6th Floor Mutual House, 70 Conduit Street, London W1S 2GF

www.unbound.com

ISBN (eBook): 978-1-911586-20-3

ISBN (Paperback):978-1-911586-19-7

Design by Mecob

Cover image:

© Shutterstock.com
© iStockphoto.com

This book was produced using Pressbooks.com, and PDF rendering was done by PrinceXML.

For Jenny, my muse.

Dear Reader,

The book you are holding came about in a rather different way to most others. It was funded directly by readers through a new website: Unbound.

Unbound is the creation of three writers. We started the company because we believed there had to be a better deal for both writers and readers. On the Unbound website, authors share the ideas for the books they want to write directly with readers. If enough of you support the book by pledging for it in advance, we produce a beautifully bound special subscribers' edition and distribute a regular edition and e-book wherever books are sold, in shops and online.

This new way of publishing is actually a very old idea (Samuel Johnson funded his dictionary this way). We're just using the internet to build each writer a network of patrons. Here, at the back of this book, you'll find the names of all the people who made it happen.

Publishing in this way means readers are no longer just passive consumers of the books they buy, and authors are free to write the books they really want. They get a much fairer return too – half the profits their books generate, rather than a tiny percentage of the cover price.

If you're not yet a subscriber, we hope that you'll want to join our publishing revolution and have your name listed in one of our books in the future. To get you started, here is a £5 discount on your first pledge. Just visit unbound.com, make your pledge and type HELMQVIST in the promo code box when you check out.

Thank you for your support,

Dan, Justin and John
Founders, Unbound

Super Patrons

Jason Bradley
Jenny Bragg
Elizabeth Bragg
Richard W H Bray
Natia Breedlove
Mr Buttons
Michael Carpenter
Steven Davies
Gareth Fernie
Barry Flaga
Göthe & Maria Götesson
Paul Holbrook
Marty Lowell Keeter
Dan Kieran
Erika Lindsay
Ted Milliner
John Mitchinson
Gun-Britt & Morgan Öhman
Bengt Oskarsson
Kerstin Oskarsson
Marissa Parkin
David & Karen Pinkston
Justin Pollard
Scott Reid
Kevin Sullivan
David G Tubby
Tom Woodgate

With grateful thanks to David and Karen Pinkston

Author's Note

A personal dedication in the front of the novel was one of the reward levels offered during the funding campaign for *Transilience*. Only one dedication was offered and you can imagine my delight when my parents scooped it up at the first opportunity.

This novel could not have happened without them. They possess the best qualities a child would wish in their parents. They have given me unconditional support. They believe in my work and me. And they have the highest of hopes that I will succeed in any, and all, of my endeavours. I am very lucky to have them in my life.

So, Mom and Dad, thank you. Thank you for helping me to realise a dream. Thank you for helping me on my journey to become a published author. And thank you for being such great parents.

Your son,
Kevin

Transilience

(*Noun*) An abrupt change or variation; (*adjective*) leaping or passing from one thing or state to another. Etymology: Latin *transiliens*, present participle of *transilire*, to leap across or over.

1

New London, Mars

The 3rd Street Lounge is a swanky bar in the city's hellhole: the Industrial/Manufacturing District. The owner, Curtis, transformed an abandoned cube of a building into a classy gin joint with a stage for swinging bands, a dance floor for the uninhibited, an island bar in the centre of the room for the thirsty, small tables near the stage for the enthusiastic and cosy booths along the wall for the intimate. Imported wood and Art Deco comprise the majority of the decor. Why Curt chose the IM, and how he paid for the place (or the renovations for that matter), is beyond me. I've never asked because I don't care.

Anywhere else in New London, the 3rd Street Lounge would be packed every weekday night and have a line around the block on weekends. Anywhere else in this city, bands would be begging to get a gig. Instead, the stage has never seen a live act and the only people lining up are the factory workers who go to the bar instead of home at the end of their shifts.

I had my usual booth along the wall near the dance floor, and was kept company by the remnants of a gin and tonic. Baseball highlights streamed on my MIX12. If I hadn't been so oblivious to the world around me, I'd have seen her walk in, looking as out of place in this joint as a herd of elephants on the *Elysium Planitia*.

I only glanced up when I heard my name and caught a glimpse of the one person who could send me through the wormhole. At that moment, flight became impossible. Instead, I sat, rooted in my booth, and gaped like a fool at a woman who'd have made the Judgement of Paris infinitely harder.

Now, don't get me wrong; I'm not one of those poor saps

instantly smitten by any dame that crosses my path. There are plenty of good-looking women in New London. But not like her. She possessed the kind of class only the truly beautiful enjoy, the very image of a New Look model complete with an Arden-styled jacket. The deep forest-green tones of the fabric matched the shade of her eyes. A blonde pixie cut framed a determined jaw, angular cheekbones and a perfectly shaped nose.

As the mystery woman glided towards me, her expression radiated contempt. I guess I couldn't blame her. Instead of sitting in my office, I was entrenched in a booth in New London's very own industrial nightmare, watching sport highlights and clutching a near-empty highball glass.

Despite what I might say on the subject, first impressions matter. The thought of being viewed as some common wino stung like a punch to the gut.

I extracted myself from my spot and rose to greet her. She checked me out again – this time head to toe. Fortunately, my pressed wool suit and tidy haircut stood in contrast to the other patrons of the bar. Add to that my 185 centimetres of fighting fitness, and I almost made inroads. A slight smile implied a minor success.

'You are Daniel Helmqvist?' she asked with a girlish voice that betrayed the smooth, silvery tone I had already conjured in my mind.

'I am. Would you care to sit and may I take your coat?'

She arched a pencil thin eyebrow. 'Take my coat?'

'Yeah. You know, help you out of it and hang it up?'

She turned her back to me.

'A guy who takes a lady's coat. What century did you step out of?'

She couldn't see my shrug or my lop-sided grin. 'I descend from a long line of Helmqvists who put a premium on politeness.'

'Polite? What a rarity these days,' she replied as I slid off her cashmere trench coat to reveal shapely shoulders and arms of flawless alabaster. A coat hanger attached to the booth gave me the option to do more than just toss it on the bench seat.

Unexpectedly she sat down in the exact spot I had vacated only seconds ago. The confusion killed the moment of witty banter I had been enjoying with this stranger.

'Can, umm, can I get you anything?'

'A soda water with a twist of lemon.'

'Coming right up.'

A few minutes later, I slid around to the bend of the U-shaped booth with her drink in my left hand and a G&T in my right.

'Now, Miss—'

'Rennick.'

'To what do I owe this visit?' I asked as I pulled my MIX12 and trilby to my side of the table.

'I wish to hire your services on a very delicate matter.'

'I have an office where I usually meet prospective clients.'

'Your assistant directed me to this place when I called your business number.'

Of course she did... 'Wonderful. Okay, well you're here now. What's the job?'

Her emerald eyes flicked towards the door before settling on mine. She seemed far too distracted and worried for my comfort. I fought an overwhelming urge to glance in that same direction.

'Does the name Paul Fischer ring a bell?'

I went for the obvious answer: 'The guy convicted and sent up the river for blowing up the UN building, most of East Side Manhattan and tens of thousands of people? What about him?'

'What if I told you that he had been set up? That he unwittingly took the fall for the crime?'

I shrugged. 'The Attorney General made a good case against him and the twelve people sitting in the jury box agreed with his argument. But let's skip the hypothetical. You think someone else did it, right?'

'No, I *know* someone else did it.' Her gaze flashed past me once again.

'Are you expecting someone, Miss Rennick?'

'I have taken a considerable risk coming here.'

I turned my head and stared at the entrance as if a couple of hard boys would come crashing through right at that moment. No one did. The Quantic remix of Skalpel's '1958' filled the brief lull in our conversation.

I took a long pull at my highball and sat the half-empty glass down. 'Please continue.'

'Someone else planned the attack and planted a trail of evidence that led straight to Paul Fischer.'

'You sound pretty confident.'

She sipped her club soda. 'I am.'

'Despite the fact that they had overwhelming proof of his involvement in the bombing – eyewitness accounts, video corroboration and a laptop with a recovered copy of the manifesto sent out afterwards on it?'

She nodded. 'Doesn't that sound a little too convenient? At best, all it means is the culprit gave the investigators just enough information to string them along until Fischer became the one obvious suspect.'

I finished my drink. 'Why not go to the police, or contact the FBI, or the Attorney General's Office in New York?'

'They would never believe me and I would be exposed to the very person I am trying to hide this from.' She paused and let out a measured sigh. 'You see, it involves someone far too important for the police to even consider them capable of mass murder.'

I glanced down at my highball glass, wishing it hadn't run dry. 'Who is this person?' I managed at last.

She looked up and our eyes met: 'Mara Kitterman.'

'The same Mara Kitterman who put our city on the galactic map!?'

Charlotte looked around to ensure no one had heard.

'You can see why I cannot go to the authorities, right? They would never believe me.'

'Lady, I'm not even sure I believe you. Mass murder is pretty far down the list of things I think Mara Kitterman would do. What proof do you have?'

'A datapad exists that contains all of the information required to prosecute her.' A hint of defiance tinted the edge of Rennick's voice.

'I don't suppose you know where it is, do you? For that matter, how do you even know it exists?'

'If I knew its location, I wouldn't need you. As far as *how* I know, let's just say that I have overheard things that give weight to my belief in her guilt.'

The conversation lapsed again. I glanced at her while she picked at a beer coaster. Mara Kitterman, a killer. A ridiculous notion. But intriguing nonetheless.

'Do you believe me?'

'Not really.'

'What if I paid you to look into it anyway?' Her attention was back on me now.

'I'd feel bad taking your money.'

'It's my money. I'll spend it as I like.'

'Fine, but let me ask you this: if she did do it, why go after her now?'

'It is a secret I have borne for too long,' she whispered, so quietly that I almost missed it.

I leaned in closer to her, thrown off by the gravity of her response.

She nodded her head towards Curtis. 'Besides, I'm certain you have a healthy bar tab to pay off. Look into it and see what you uncover. If, at the end of two weeks, you haven't discovered anything, we settle up and go our separate ways. If, however, you *do* discover something to support my claims, we see this through to the end. Is that a deal?'

I gave the question the customary amount of thinking. 'I'll give you two solid weeks of investigation. If, by some wild stretch of the imagination, your allegation has a kernel of truth, then I'll be your man to the end.'

Her pert lips formed an imperceptible smile.

'My rate is five hundred credits a day plus expenses.'

'Perfectly reasonable. Now, if you will excuse me, I must go before I am missed at work.'

She scooted out of the booth and I scrambled to follow. Once standing, we exchanged business cards. She grabbed her coat and made for the door. I glanced down at her details:

Charlotte Rennick
Applied Science Division
MARA Corporation,
1 Corporation South, Research District 1
Tel: (1601) 21274962
Email: charlotte.rennick@maracorp.mrs

'I will call you in a few days to see how you are progressing,' she called out before stepping into the strong Martian daylight.

And, like that, she vanished. I stood there, long after the door had closed, lost in thought. Curt's voice shook me from my reverie.

'What the hell was that all about?'

I sidled up to the bar. 'Can't say.'

'Can't or won't?'

A grin on his face.

'Both.'

'Another gin and tonic, then?'

My attention drifted back to the door. 'Make it a double, I've got some serious thinking to do.'

2

With my drink in hand, I didn't even make it back to my booth before my MAX smartwatch began to vibrate. I checked the display. It read, 'Unknown'.

'Daniel Helmqvist,' I answered after fishing my earpiece out of my front trouser pocket with my free hand and tapping a green button on the watch face.

'Good afternoon. My name is Samuel Porter of HTS Intergalactic.' His plummy upper-crust British accent nearly caused me to choke on the sip of gin I had just taken.

'What can I do for you?'

'I wonder if you could come down to my office and discuss a business proposition?'

'I usually meet potential clients in my office, Mr Porter. It's one of the reasons I pay the rent on the place.'

'Naturally,' he replied after another short pause. 'However, your assistant informed me you were out of your office and not likely to return for the day.' I detected a theme in the interruption of my afternoon. 'And in any event,' he continued, 'I had hoped you would make an exception. There is something that I need to show you, but I dare not do so in any place other than my office.'

Now he had me intrigued.

'Alright, Mr Porter. I'll be there within the hour.'

'Do you know the location of our corporate offices?'

'I assume you're on Mars. The rest I can figure out on the way.'

'Give reception your name. They will be expecting you.'

'Right. See you shortly.'

We both rang off the line.

I drained the contents of my highball, grabbed my things and directed my feet to the nearest subway station.

On the way, I dug up as much detail as I could on Porter and HTS from the web. High Temperature Superconductors (HTS) Intergalactic did exactly what the name implied they did: built super-conductors. The company owned a flashy headquarters in Research District 2 and their main production facility occupied real estate in the IM. They also had offices and factories sprinkled throughout the known systems. Samuel Porter served as the company's CEO and had done so for the last two decades.

Forty-five minutes later, I strolled through a pair of glass doors into a spacious, atrium-style lobby. Light flooded through the glass walls and ceiling to cast a warm glow on a myriad of displayed products made by HTS Intergalactic. Down the middle of all this ran a wide carpet to a massive reception desk.

'Welcome to HTS Intergalactic. How may I be of assistance?' asked a tasty piece of set decoration sitting at the desk.

I sized her up. It took me a few seconds to realise she wasn't made of flesh and bones. An ultra-realistic model. Must have cost Porter a mint.

'I'm here to see Mr Porter. The name is Daniel Helmqvist.'

'Of course. One moment.' She typed something into her computer. 'Mr Porter will be right down. Please make yourself comfortable.' She motioned to a nearby armchair.

I settled into one of two thick-cushioned Lawsons, grabbed a MIX13 from a nearby table and skimmed through all of the 'innovative products and services provided by HTS Intergalactic'. Samuel Porter called my name as he approached.

Coming towards me, he checked in a shade over 180 centimetres tall and between 80 and 85 kilos. His bald head reflected the afternoon sun with a waxy brilliance. He wore a bespoke dark navy suit with a silk waistcoat and a matching patterned tie.

I stood up to greet him.

We shook hands. 'Nice place you have here.'

'Thank you, Mr Helmqvist. Business has been good to us lately,' Porter replied with that odd butler inflection I had heard over the phone. 'Would you please follow me?'

Porter led me to his office on the top floor of the three-storey building. On our way, we passed his personal assistant. Definitely human, and very easy on the eyes. Before I had a chance to make an introduction, he ushered me through a set of thick, wooden double doors and offered me a seat at an executive conference table.

'Can I offer you something to drink?'

'A gin and—'

In my peripheral, I caught a glimpse of an antique gallery wall clock. Neither hand pointed to Happy Hour. I checked myself and cleared my throat.

'A cup of coffee. Milk. No sugar, please.'

'Right.'

He eyed me with caution. I clearly had gin on my mind and it did not go unnoticed.

While we waited for his assistant to bring my coffee and Porter's cup of tea, he grabbed a MIX13 from his desk and took a seat next to me. He opened up a few documents on the computer and was about to send them to a holographic display when the arrival of our drinks interrupted him. He flipped the tablet over to cover the screen with a look of mild panic. Strange reaction.

Once we were alone again, Porter leaned in and dropped his voice down to a level best described as conspiratorial. 'What I am about to show you, Mr Helmqvist, is very private and very damning. However, I've been assured that you are an honest man with a great deal of integrity. So I can trust your discretion, yes?'

'Who told you that about me?'

'The District Attorney.'

'You know him?'

'We play golf once a week.'

By playing golf, Porter meant swinging a stick at a screen and chasing after a digital ball. Because the Martian environment is not conducive to the real thing, enthusiasts climb into sophisticated, immersive VR chambers and play any number of famous courses. They create clubs around these machines and even hire architects to design new courses for them. Rich people...

'And I came up in a conversation?'

'I called him this morning and asked if he knew of anyone good at solving problems… other than the police.'

'And he gave you my name?'

'He did, indeed.'

'Heh, who knew?' I asked rhetorically with a slight chuckle. 'Anyway, you can trust me.'

'Right,' he said dismissively, once again. 'As I was saying, this is a sensitive issue for me.'

Porter flipped the MIX13 back over, opened his email and sent a message from earlier this morning to the holographic display set in the centre of the conference table.

Embedded into the email was a video. When Porter began to play it, a factory tucked away in a tropical forest faded into view.

The video looked to be taken at a distance but the zoom capability allowed for some detailed close-ups. The images on the screen appeared to be the business end of a mining operation or mineral processing plant. The video went on for several minutes and then went blank.

A second later, the screen became a blur of images, moving too fast for me to process. Between the flashes of images and, at times, transposed over them, words appeared that looked like they had been cut out of a magazine – like some crazy ransom note.

Pillage
Plunder
Death
Destruction
Genocide

And so on and so forth.

The screen dissolved into nothingness. After maybe a second, words materialised once more in a blood red script that oozed down the screen.

Naughty, naughty, HTS! We know your dirty little secret.

After a few seconds, the sentences faded away and were replaced by something I had never seen before.

3

A bipedal creature, covered in a soft, green mossy fur, filled the entire screen. On first glance, it bore a strong resemblance to the Great Apes found on Earth – long, muscular arms, short powerful legs, thick torso, sloping cranium and elongated muzzle.

However, upon closer inspection, a few differences took the beast out of the zoo and placed it firmly in the imagination of Verne. It had a third limb under its left arm. A three-jointed scraggly-looking appendage with an extra digit on the hand. Dagger-like teeth filled the creature's mouth. Definitely not made for munching on bananas. And its eyes looked more arachnid than mammalian. I believe the technical term for it was creepy as hell.

The image faded again and another message arranged itself on the screen.

> We know what you've done.
> Twenty million credits buys our silence.
> Be ready to transfer the money by midnight UTC, Saturday.
> If not, we go public.
> We will contact you soon with the transfer details.

'What the hell was that thing!?'

'It is the native species on the planet *Ithilles*,' Porter replied. 'We have named them *thillians*.'

'Who is "we"?'

'HTS Intergalactic.'

'Since when do you get to name species?'

'Since we were the only ones who knew about them until now.'

'Aside from the obvious blackmailing that's going on here, I'm lost. Care to elaborate?'

After a couple of minutes of uncomfortable silence, Samuel Porter began to speak in a slow, deliberate manner. He sounded like a professor I once had in undergrad.

'As you may know, when the group, Innominate, leaked all of the technical documentation on a Faster Than Light programme developed by the United States – colloquially known as Space Folding – humanity entered a type of Space Race unrivalled by the previous centuries. Since the information became public against their wishes, the US government decided to make the technology available to anyone clever enough to build a ship that could use it without fear of legal retribution.'

He took a breath and a sip of his tea. I waited patiently for what I knew was coming. What every kid learns in school as soon as they are old enough to read.

'Any corporation with enough capital to invest in Space Folding did so,' he continued. 'Thousands of companies poured millions of credits into devising a propulsion system, which could take them anywhere in the galaxy in a matter of seconds. The results were chaos. Ships crewed by hundreds vanished, never to return. Rights to ownership of Earth-like planets disputed. Can a corporation, or a country for that matter, claim an entire planet as their own? If not, how much ownership of a planet could they claim? In response to these questions and incidents, the United Nations passed Security Council Resolution 10191, which established the Galactic Court.'

I couldn't be certain this was ever going to end but nothing seems to be more energising to an old man than a captive audience.

'In an unparalleled show of solidarity, every country on the Council,' Porter waxed on, 'recognised the Court's authority as a mediator in all matters beyond the atmosphere of the Earth and exploration of the galaxy continued. As FTL technology became cheaper and more reliable, travel to places once before thought to be impossible became possible. The base level of knowledge and understanding of our universe grew exponentially. New materials were discovered.

New species of flora and fauna. In fact, one such find, Gravitronium, allowed New London to grow from the tiny research outpost that is now the Spaceport to the wonderful metropolis we have today—'

I couldn't take it anymore and snapped. 'Yes, yes! I do know! I know a substratum of Gravitronium laid down far under the surface of New London has given us a near 1g environment within the domes. We have the joy of living like Earthlings without the benefit of breathable air. I know all of this because everyone knows this—'

Porter looked annoyed at me cutting him off and launching into a diatribe. I needed to calm myself.

Serenity now. Serenity now. I chanted to myself a few times.

'What I don't understand – or rather have the patience to wait to find out – is what this has to do with Ithilles and those green monsters.'

'Ithilles and the thillians are HTS's greatest secret.'

'Well, you boys have done a pretty good job of keeping quiet. I didn't even think it was possible to find a planet with life on it without anyone else knowing.'

'I suppose we are fortunate in that regard.'

'What's so special about it?'

'Our research and development group found Ithilles nearly three decades ago. We've kept it a secret because the planet contains a very valuable resource.'

'Where's it located?'

'In a system about forty-two light years from here, within the constellation *Ophiuchus*. We stumbled upon it quite by accident and discovered it had all the necessary conditions to support life, as we know it. However, we also discovered the planet was already inhabited.'

'The ape-looking thing?'

'Yes, Mr Helmqvist, among other lesser life forms, but the thillians were the dominant species on the planet. Despite their being a primitive sort of hominid, they possessed a crude form of social hierarchy and limited technology use. Moreover, their resemblance to the apes on Earth is remarkable and might have some larger implication.'

He paused to take another sip of his tea.

'However, one thing that is fascinating,' he continued after he placed his cup back on its saucer, 'is that their centres of power are all located in, or around, the ruins of some other ancient civilisation. We have found crumbling remains that suggest Ithilles was once populated by a much more advanced race of peoples, for lack of a better term. Whether the thillians killed them off, a natural disaster subsumed them, or they simply died out we do not know.'

'So are these thillians the resource you mentioned?'

'Oh no. Not in the least. They have some curious physiological aspects to their development but they are just that – a curiosity.'

'Then what are you after?'

'Are you familiar with the compound yttrium?'

'Rare earth metal used primarily in the manufacturing of super conductors.'

Porter raised an eyebrow in surprise. 'Very good, Mr Helmqvist. Then you also know that it is becoming increasingly difficult to find on Earth and rarely found as a free element.'

I nodded.

'We discovered it in abundance on Ithilles – as a free element no less. Entire pristine veins of the mineral waiting for someone with the means and the determination to pull it out of the ground.'

'Sounds like a windfall for your company, Porter.'

'Indeed. Almost too good to be true.'

'And let me guess, the thillians weren't too keen on you setting up a mining operation?'

'Sadly, no. They are an aggressive, territorial species. As soon as a company ship touched down on the planet, they attacked the landing party. Only a handful made it off Ithilles alive.'

'So you sent a private army there to secure it by force?'

'That's correct. After the fate of the first group, we did not want to make the same mistake twice.'

'Mass extermination?'

Porter closed his eyes and bobbed his head up and down.

'Genocide on a planet known only to HTS just to get your hands on some raw material?'

'Regrettably, yes.'

'You seem awfully contrite for someone waist deep in this whole business.' I fought hard to keep the anger burning in my chest at bay. Corporate greed. A story as old as civilisation itself.

Discovery of a new planet with a new species and their subsequent elimination was a lot to take in. I began to wish in earnest that the cup of coffee in front of me had a slug of whisky in it.

'I assure you, Mr Helmqvist, I am not proud of my company's past but it is a legacy that I inherited.'

'Why not pull out and be done with it?' I asked, trying to regain control of my emotions.

'Our production, our profits, everything depends on cheap access to yttrium. To leave would be financial ruin. A lot of people's livelihoods are at stake.'

'How many people know about your operation on Ithilles?'

'The company's executive board. The facilities manager. Two members of our Applied Science division. And the head of our private security detail.'

'I'm guessing your security detail are all synthetics?'

Porter nodded again. No loyalty issues there. 'Roughly then, what? Ten people?'

'Fourteen to be exact.'

Enough for a leak, especially if someone grew a conscience.

'How trustworthy are the ones who know the history of the planet?'

'They all have a considerable financial stake in the company and I know each one personally. Twenty million is not *that* great a sum to them.'

Must be nice. 'Care to tell me where the footage came from?'

'It is archived footage an HTS team took soon after the occupation of the planet. These blackmailers found a way into our computer system and stole the recordings.'

'Why on Earth would you even keep anything like that? I'm surprised it took this long for someone to find it.'

'Sometimes these things slip through the cracks and subduing the planet happened before my time, which always made it, more or less, an abstraction to me. Anyway, it can't be helped now.'

I shook my head at his deference. The annihilation of species slipping through the cracks like he forgot to buy milk at the grocery store. 'Who else in the company knows about this email?' I asked instead.

'I am not sure, Mr Helmqvist. However, I believe that you and I are the only ones aware of it.'

'Let's hope you're right. If this thing goes public, you're looking at some pretty serious charges from the Galactic Court. You and everyone else with firsthand knowledge. Your associates could do something rash.'

'That is preposterous! Even if they were moved to violence, killing me would hardly solve their problems.'

'It might or it might not.' I shrugged. 'What I do know is that if you are dead, they can pin all kinds of horrible things on you and you can't deny them.'

'Not necessarily, Mr Helmqvist. This all took place well before my time as head of the company.'

'Is that a risk you're willing to take? A staged suicide with a note explaining your role in the perpetuation of this secret. Disgust with who you've become. Goodbye cruel world. If done right, your death wouldn't even warrant an investigation. Seems plausible to me. The rest would be damage control for the other members of the board. Corporations have survived worse.'

He tensed up. 'I am certain these blackmailers have contacted no one else. If so, I would already know about it.'

The conversation lapsed as I tried to process everything. After a few minutes, Porter broke the silence.

'Will you take the case?'

I restarted the video. 'I need a few more minutes to think about it.'

The images and the text flowed past my eyes. All the while I weighed the benefits of doing business with a man like Porter against my conscience. By the end of the video, the scales were clearly tipped towards 'the benefits of doing business'. In my line of work, high-minded platitudes didn't pay the bills.

'I'll take the job.'

'Splendid! When can you start and what is your fee?'

To my surprise, I didn't regurgitate my usual spiel immediately after he popped the question. Instead I swung for the fences. 'Ten thousand.'

'Ten thousand per day?'

'Too low?'

'Quite the contrary! Do you always charge this much? If so, it's a wonder you have any clients at all.'

'Nah, usually my rates are pretty reasonable. I'm making an exception here. But I tell you what, if I don't solve this case before you have to pay the blackmail, I'll waive my fee.'

'How very generous of you.'

I stood and grabbed my coat and hat. 'Think of it this way: it's a bargain compared to twenty mil.'

4

Outside HTS, I hailed the first free cab to come my way and hopped in.

'Where to, mister?' asked a red-headed baritone who looked too young, and too skinny, to be wearing a voice that deep.

'5021 Tireman, Commercial District.'

He punched the address into his navigation system. Even without getting a good look at him, I knew right away he was human. Android cabbies had a built-in navigation unit and, consequently, were liberated from the need to go through the same rituals as this guy. An android never struggled with getting lost.

We drove in silence, and I used the time to reflect on my meeting with Porter. The window for this case was pretty tight, and a successful outcome rested largely on the assumption that the blackmailers lived on Mars. This aspect of the case never came up in the meeting, and I didn't want to press it because I needed the credits. If they did live somewhere else in the galaxy, all I could do was pass along the info to Porter and hope he got to them before they went public – and that he'd still pay me when the dust settled.

'Any reason someone would be following us?'

'Following us? What?'

'A metallic blue Electroglide has been tailing us since I picked you up.'

I shifted in my seat to get a better look out the back window. 'That's not an Electroglide!' I shouted out like some halfwit.

'Nah, two cars behind us,' he replied, graciously overlooking my statement of the obvious.

I caught a glimpse of the car, driven by a guy in a flat cap and a pair of aviators, at the exact moment it made a left at the first intersection inside the Commercial District.

Immediately, I had my earpiece in and dialled my office.

'Pam!' I barked as soon as I heard 'hello'.

'Yes, sir?'

'I need you to access the street cameras in Commercial in the vicinity of Brush and Harper. Look for a metallic blue Electroglide, single driver, male, and wearing a cap and sunglasses. I'm only a few blocks away. You can fill me in when I get there.'

'Yes, sir,' she replied automatically.

'Would you like me to try to catch the 'glide?' my driver asked after I rang off the line. 'It shouldn't be too difficult.'

'Tempting, but I am pressed for time.' However, in the excitement of the moment, I leaned closer to the partition separating the front and back of the cabin. 'How did you know we had someone following us? The Electroglide must be one of the most popular models on this rock.'

'I spend all day driving these roads. Most of the time seeing it through my rearview and side cameras.' He paused for a moment, trying to find the words. 'I guess it's just something I've picked up. The same make and colour car with the same plate number, always two to three cars back. It sticks out. You know?'

I didn't know; however, I did know my esteem for the ginger chauffeur trebled. This was the kinda guy I could work with and I regarded him with newfound interest.

He turned down Tireman, my office visible at the end of the block.

The car came to a gentle stop in front. 'That'll be twenty-five credits.'

I put my right thumb on a reader mounted to the back of the driver's seat. It read the microchip embedded under my skin. A screen popped up on the partition glass that showed the amount of the fare and an option to include a tip. I added 10 credits and confirmed the total on a touch screen next to the thumb pad.

'Listen,' I said as I prepared to get out. 'I might need a wheelman in the coming days. You wouldn't want to earn a little on the side, would you?'

CHAPTER FOUR

'I dunno. It depends on the type of work, I guess.'

'Pretty straightforward. I call you and ask for a lift to some place. If you're free and you want the dough, you say, "be right there". Here.' I passed one of my business cards through a small slot in the partition.

'A private eye,' he said as he looked at it. 'You workin' on something big, Mr' – he glanced back down at the card – 'Helmqvist?'

'You can call me Dan. I can't really discuss it at the moment. But what do you think? Up for a late-night prowl if I call you?'

He slid my card into his shirt pocket. 'Sure, I could use the extra credits.'

He produced one of his own cards.

Dial-A-Taxi
Steve Davies
Tel: 1605 21872874

'Superb. I'll contact you if something comes up.'

Before I went up to my office, I had one more phone call to make.

'Hello, Danny.'

'Hey Erica. I hope I didn't call at a bad time.'

'Actually, your timing is perfect, I just finished my shift.'

'I know we have a date tomorrow…' I paused for a breath, which gave Erica enough time to interject an *oh*. Disappointment hung heavy on the line. I regrouped and ploughed on.

'But I just landed a big case. I doubt I'll be finished with it in time. Could we rebook for the day after?'

Another *oh*, but this time it conveyed a definite sense of relief. 'That works for me, Danny. In fact, it's probably better because I have Sunday off. I'll be able to stay out as long as I want and not have to suffer at work the next day.'

That last comment seemed innocent enough but certainly left the door open for possibilities.

'Great! I'll call DKY and reschedule for reservations at eight on Saturday. That sound alright?'

'Sounds perfect. Do you still have my address?'

'Ingrained in my memory.' That earned me a laugh. 'I'll pick you up around seven thirty. Cool?'

'Very much so. Bye Danny.'

Erica Green worked the day shift at the nearby 24-hour auto-mated diner I frequented most days on my way to the office. She had long, black hair, high cheekbones and almond-coloured eyes a shade darker than her skin tone. Probably in her late twenties or early thir-ties at a stretch. I never asked out of politeness. We had been flirting with each other for months before I finally grew a pair and asked her out. Figures it'd fall in the middle of this new case. Saturday might have been a gamble. I'd have either nailed the blackmailers, and had a reason to celebrate. Or, I'd have failed to find them, and had a cause for commiseration.

Polished metal framed a frosted glass door stencilled with my name, vocation and telephone number in thick, black copperplate. The dreary eggshell white walls surrounding the door radiated uninspired monotony. Amber Martian ceramic tiles covered the hallway floor and spilled into my office. The combination of walls and tiles gave the place a clinical feel.

The opaque door softened the light coming into the hallway from the reception area. I watched the blurred figure of Pam, my office assistant, working at her desk. She glanced up as I entered before resuming her typing. I sat down on the edge of her desk and dropped my trilby on my right knee.

'Hi Pam. Any luck on the Electroglide?'

'Between his speed and erratic behaviour, the driver violated approximately twelve different traffic laws. I managed to grab his plate number, though.'

'And?'

'According to the Transportation Authority's database, it belongs to a Libra scheduled to be demolished, and the plate's number recycled back into the system.'

She pulled up a screen grab from one of the city's street cameras on her computer screen. Even with all of the clean-up Pam had done on the picture, the guy hid behind the bill of his flat cap and his shades. An ID would be impossible.

Stolen plates on what was most likely a stolen car driven by a stranger in a tweed hat. I had a couple of very good notions as to why he'd been tailing me, but nothing solid to go on. And I had a black-mail case to solve.

'Nice work, Pam. A few things don't add up but we'll have to let this one go.'

'Add up? I fail to see how this conversation involves maths.' She didn't mean to make a joke, but I laughed all the same. From time to time, I forgot she's an android. And despite the fact that she seemed to be acting more and more human, she didn't deal too well with some abstractions or colloquialisms. I found it an endless source of mirth but I may be the only one in the office who did.

'Figure of speech, Pam. Anyway, thanks to your meddling into my perfectly serene afternoon, I now have two cases.' I then pro-ceeded to fill in my assistant on both meetings.

'Since you can work quicker than I can, you start digging into HTS Intergalactic's board members, R&D guys, and head of security to see if you can connect any of them to the blackmail. I'll refresh my memory on the UN bombing for the Rennick case, and we'll discuss our findings in a few hours.'

'How would you like me to proceed with my task?'

'Sneak through the back door and dig into email records, employee history, anything you can think of. Check into their per-sonal lives, as well. When a company has a secret this dirty, a moun-tain of debt is usually a pretty good motive for blackmail. My guess is that someone employed there is trying to make some quick credits.'

She acknowledged by way of turning back to her computer and banging on the keys with purpose. A function completely unneces-sary for an android, but one that has become accepted practice. Most businesses, or organisations that use robots for administrative purposes, have found an android sitting at a desk, staring blankly off into space, a tad unnerving. The solution was to make them appear as human as possible, and therefore most of them have been programmed to use a keyboard. Pam, however, has turned keyboard use into a new art form.

I settled into my office chair, fixed myself a gin and tonic from the right hand desk drawer that served as my mini bar, and began sifting through archived media reports of the UN bombing.

Five years ago, a radical group called the Galton Society claimed responsibility for setting off a small nuclear bomb at the UN's Millennial Park. The blast wiped out the entire UN complex and a sizeable chunk of Manhattan's Lower East Side. In the 24 hours between the explosion and the time it took for the previously unheard of Galton Society to take credit, Earth descended into pandemonium. Were it not for the manifesto sent out by the Society and the subsequent arrest of Paul Fischer, a high-powered DC lobbyist with a beef against immigrants in the US, I had no doubt that humanity would have destroyed itself.

However, the feds caught a couple of lucky breaks. First, they managed to pull UN surveillance video from a cloud server that showed Fischer entering the UN about 30 minutes before the explosion. Using facial recognition software, the feds also found images of him at various locations in Manhattan leading up to the blast. And the icing on the cake: they found him in his room at the Four Seasons, which happened to be outside the destruction zone. They booked him as suspect numero uno.

The second break came when FBI techs cracked the encryption on his laptop and found a copy of the Galton Society's manifesto on his hard drive. The manifesto called for the expulsion of all 'lesser races' from the great centres of civilisation.

Once law enforcement had a name and face to go with it, information about Fischer came in thick and fast. At trial, eyewitness testimony corroborated the video footage and a series of digital trails all pointed to Fischer being in Manhattan without a clear objective. His defence argued he was there to meet a potential donor but could not supply supporting evidence. Purported phone conversations, a plane ticket, and the hotel room being paid for by this mystery person all led right back to Fischer, himself.

The case against Paul Fischer may have not been a slam-dunk, but it didn't really matter in the end. He looked like a guilty man, the AG had enough to pin him to the scene of the crime and a jury agreed.

Fortunately, I was saved from any more reading by Pam's voice over the intercom.

'Sir, I believe I've found something.'

'Great, come into my office and we'll discuss it.'

In she came and sat in a tired, old armchair facing my desk.

'Okay, Pam, tell me what you've got.'

'I found a virus attached to a copy of Samuel Porter's updated schedule that his office assistant sent to him at the start of the work day.'

'His office assistant? Seems a tad clichéd doesn't it?'

'I am not certain how to answer that, sir. However, the virus itself was an effective means to her ends. When Mr Porter dumped the schedule into his calendar, the virus propagated to all of his other devices once he synchronised them, making it difficult to track back to the original source.'

'Clever girl. What's her name?'

'Lyric Voss.'

5

Because of Pam's success at finding the culprit behind the blackmail video, and my failure to unearth anything interesting with the UN bombing, I was immediately struck with an urge to take over Pam's share of the workload.

'Find anything new in your search?' she asked, as if reading my mind.

'Nothing. I have no reason to believe anyone other than Fischer blew up the UN five years ago. I have messages left at the AG's office in New York and with a reporter who covered the attack and subsequent trial, but that's all I've got. Unreturned messages and nothing anyone couldn't find with a quick internet search.'

My assistant stared at me.

'What, Pam?'

'Based on my calculations, there is an eighty-eight per cent chance that Paul Fischer was innocent.'

'Eighty-eight per cent?'

'I rounded to the nearest whole number, sir.'

'Why don't you think he did it?'

'That is a complicated question.'

'Enlighten me.' I rocked back in my chair, highball glass in my hand, prepared to listen to the insights of an android.

'Paul Fischer lacked the means and the motive to carry out an event such as the UN bombing.'

'He hated immigrants,' I reminded her. 'He spent his entire professional career trying to kick them out of the US.'

'He had no history of violence, sir. No arrest records. No known association with violent xenophobic organisations. Nothing to suggest he was capable of, or willing to use, violence. His *modi operandi* involved lobbying for legislative changes and supporting candidates who shared his ideology.'

'First time for everything. Not to mention they had video evidence of him walking into the place with a backpack.'

'And now we move to means. Based on everything I have read about the case and Mr Fischer, he did not possess the technical skills to build a small nuclear device capable of avoiding detection by UN security officials. Naturally, he could have hired someone to build it for him, but that does not change the fact that law enforcement officials did not find any evidence of contact with radioactive materials. He passed through a security check without issue.'

'None of this exonerates him.'

'Even if one concedes he took a bomb into the UN compound, how did he survive the blast? His movements prior to his entrance are well documented, and show too much indifference to surveillance cameras to be suspicious. However, not one camera caught him exiting. Did he sneak out and set it off remotely?'

'Perhaps he used this to his advantage. You know, let everyone think you are there to throw off suspicion and then sneak out undetected,' I interjected.

'If that were the case, why did he stay in Manhattan and increase his chances of being caught? Why would he even place himself at the blast zone, clearly in harm's way, only to appear somewhere else? As I said before, it's sloppy on his part if he had designs on not being caught. Logic would dictate that he either disguised his appearance so that he could flee the scene undetected, or he died in the blast. I contend he did not know he was being implicated.'

'And from this, you've arrived at only a twelve per cent probability of his guilt?'

'That is correct, sir.'

'Who do you think did it? Mara Kitterman?'

Pam furrowed her brow in thought. 'Yes, and no. The responsible party was more likely Nolan Kitterman than Mara—'

'Nolan... What?' I cut her off. Pam hates to be cut off. Her expression gave clear indication of that. I continued. 'He'd been dead for, like, five years when the attack happened. How could you even possibly think it was him?'

'Because the attack bears a remarkable resemblance to a series of bombings on Earth, which happened twenty years ago, for which I have a theory Nolan Kitterman was responsible.'

I nearly choked on my gin. 'You have a *theory*?'

'Yes, sir.'

'This should be good. Let's hear it.'

'With respect to these earlier attacks, unlike Mr Fischer, Nolan Kitterman possessed the technical knowledge, the financial means and the irrational hatred of immigrants required to accomplish the feat.'

The 'feat' was a series of dirty bombings targeted at power plants and bridges in nine different countries about two decades ago. Another racist group, using similar language to the Galton Manifesto, claimed responsibility and vowed to strike again if the West did not revise their attitude towards allowing members of less prosperous countries inside their borders.

'Explain, please.'

'When Nolan Kitterman's wife died, he demonstrated a notable change in his behaviour.'

Albanian gangsters had gunned down Beatrice Kitterman in the middle of the street during a shoot-out with London Metro Police. In the aftermath, he went apeshit and started calling for the forcible removal of all non-British people from the island. When his ranting fell on deaf ears, he took four-year-old Mara and disappeared behind the thick walls of a Northern Ireland estate, never to be seen again until his funeral.

'Anger does not a killer make,' I offered in the guise of witty retort.

'You cannot argue that he acted like a rational human being in the aftermath of Mrs Kitterman's death.'

'I concede your point.'

'Good. Couple his anger with his frustration over elected officials ignoring his pleas for mass expulsion, the knowledge he possessed as a nuclear physicist and his substantial wealth, I argue he was behind the original bombings.'

'Again, why not Fischer? He would have been in his twenties and more than capable of doing the deed.'

'Fischer was a graduate economics student accumulating a substantial amount of loan debt to pay for his tuition at a private university in Chicago. He had neither the financial means nor the intellectual capacity to orchestrate destruction on that scale.'

'Surely others were equally capable?'

'Naturally, which is why I believe Nolan Kitterman escaped justice. He had positioned himself perfectly so as not to raise suspicion, given the parameters of the event. Not once did his name come up as a potential suspect. Others were questioned. The authorities even arrested one person, but did not have enough evidence to formally charge him. By the way, his name was not Paul Fischer. Skip ahead to five years ago, a similar bombing occurs, using similar materials and a similar manifesto is sent out in the aftermath. Based on these points, and disregarding the state of Nolan Kitterman's mortality, he is the likely candidate for the attack.'

'But we can't ignore the fact that he is dead. Dead men don't tell tales, but they also don't blow up buildings and send out manifestos. So, does that mean you believe Rennick's claim that another Kitterman is behind the UN bombing? Is that the "yes" part of your yes and no answer?'

Pam nodded. 'Pathological evidence suggests it is possible. In any event, I was merely answering your original question of whether or not Fischer "did it". Your investigation into Mara Kitterman should prove the validity of Ms Rennick's assertions.'

'Pathological evidence?'

Pam nodded. 'I have read several studies that indicate an above-average correlation between character defects in parents and the appropriation of those flaws by their offspring.'

'We have a saying for that, Pam: "like father, like son."'

'Or daughter, in this case.'

I smiled. 'True.'

'It is unfortunate we cannot interview Paul Fischer and learn his side of the story.'

'He's dead, right?'

'Stabbed in prison thirty-two days after his incarceration.'

'How convenient. Set the guy up, and then silence him forever once he's inside.'

Rennick's claim someone other than Paul Fischer blew up the UN sounded about 88 per cent less crazy.

In the interest of time, we shelved our discussion of the Kittermans, and the Rennick case, and returned our attentions to the blackmailers. Pam resumed her position in front of her keyboard and sent the infected file to my computer. Telefon Tel Aviv's *Fahrenheit Fair Enough* played in the background and I set to work.

The code inside the virus programme possessed a certain elegance. During my time in the Cyber Division of the Martian Forces, I had seen better but not by much. While I took my time scanning through the file, I thought it best we keep an eye on Porter's assistant.

'Pam,' I said aloud, 'I need you to access Ms Voss's phone and clone it into your communication system.'

Most androids came with built-in hardware and firmware that made them as functional as an overpriced smart phone. They could replicate every application and display a particular phone's layout on the back of their optical sensors. Anything the user did with his phone, the android would be able to duplicate. Hopefully, Voss hadn't gone to any great lengths to encrypt her device.

Meanwhile, I had a solid breakthrough in the case. Hidden as comments within a couple of lines of code, I found the architect of the virus: N00B 4554551N. Why these bozos felt the urge to sign their handiwork like some Renaissance master never made any sense to me. Now I had a name to work with and that was usually enough.

'Noob Assassin,' I said aloud, trying it on for size. 'What a terrible handle.'

'Any luck?' I hollered through my open door.

Pam telecommed back to my office. 'I have cloned Ms Voss's phone.'

I yelled while she used the phone. As dysfunctional as any office relationship.

'Was it difficult?'

'Not terribly. It only possessed a basic level of encryption installed by the service provider.'

Low-level encryption and she plans to sting her boss with blackmail? Maybe a not-so-clever girl.

'Dump her message log onto my terminal and then I have another task for you.'

The information from Porter's assistant immediately began to stream onto my display.

'What is it that you would like me to do, sir?'

'A name search: Noob Assassin. Try it both as N double-O B space A double-S A double-S I N and also capital N double-zero capital B space four double-five four double-five one capital N.'

'Anything else?' Pam asked, as if she already knew there was more.

'Focus your search on the forums for game sites. I'd start with the big competitive games.'

'Yes, sir.'

While Pam got to work finding more about Noob Assassin, I sifted through the detritus of Lyric Voss's chat logs. The woman seemed to message as much as she did anything else. One day in the texting life of Ms Voss represented a month's worth for an average person, or me at any rate.

The prospect of so much reading made me hungry. I checked my watch – nearly 6pm. We had been at it for a while. Time for some dinner.

I ordered a pulled chicken sandwich and fries from a joint in the district. While I waited, I refilled my glass and focused on the mountain of texts.

Ten minutes later, Pam announced dinner had arrived. I paid the man and collected my chow. All the while Pam scowled.

'A man's gotta eat,' I said as I made a hasty retreat to my office.

Pam did not dignify that with a response and went back to typing away on her keyboard at a furious pace.

With food in front of me and the remnants of my gin and tonic beside me, I scrolled through Voss's messages to the time Porter let me in on his company's dirty little secret. I figured if she was the twitchy type, she might notify Noob Assassin and let him, or her, know Porter had arranged an unscheduled meeting.

Sure enough, I struck gold with a string of texts all sent to a third-party message service. The name attached to the recipient was 'Chipmunk'.

Fortified by a couple of vicious attacks on my sandwich, I snuck into the servers of the messenger company Voss used. Eventually, I found an IP address for Chipmunk and traced it to a name: Alvin Cooper.

Alvin. Chipmunk. Cute.

Right around the same time I discovered the name of Lyric's presumed boyfriend, Pam chimed in over the intercom.

'Sir, I have discovered the identity of the Noob Assassin.'

'Where did you find it?'

'He is an Adamantium level player in a MOBA called *League of Legendary Heroes* and the leader of a guild called the Lords of Pain. Noob Assassin is a regular contributor to the game's official forum site.'

I knew the game but never played it, so his level didn't mean much to me. However, it was one of the most popular player versus player games in the galaxy. Every year a tournament bogged down the communication lines between solar systems and pitted each system's champion against the others' to determine a galaxy winner. It was like the Super Bowl for nerds.

'How do you spell the name of the guild?'

'L-O-R-D-Z O-F P-4-1-N,' Pam answered.

'Another terrible name,' I replied. 'This guy seems like an ass to me. Who would want to date him?'

'I am not certain that I am qualified to answer that. Would you like me to send you some of his forum posts? From what I can discern, he seems to be a troll who enjoys flaming people on the site.'

'Where did you learn how to speak like that?' I asked, laughing.

'I do a lot of research,' she answered, as her voice trailed off.

'Sorry, I didn't mean to offend you. I was surprised is all. No need to send me his forum drivel, just give me his name.'

'According to Noob Assassin's account information, his real name is Alvin Cooper.'

Bingo! We have a match.

'Does he have a billing address on his account?'

'Yes, sir. 314D Berkshire Street, Residential District 3.'

'Did you confirm it with the city directory?'

'Naturally. It is a match.'

Little did Alvin know, this witch-doctor made house calls.

6

The rest of the night passed rather quickly, or at least what I remembered of it. Pam and I had dug up quite a bit on Mr Cooper. He was 24, above average grades, and paid his rent through an IT support job and competitive video games.

He lived in one of the poorer areas of Residential District 3, which said something because the whole damn place looked like the set for a zombie movie. He also had a roommate. Luther Dwerry worked on a line at one of the factories in the neighbouring Industrial/Manufacturing District.

Pam nudged me into the waking world before adjusting the dimness setting on the smart-glass windows. Sunlight filled the room.

'Good morning, sir,' she said, with what might have been a hint of kindness in her tone. I checked my watch: 10 minutes before noon.

I wiped the sleep from my eyes and discovered a cup of Joe and a bagel on my desk. 'Thank you for the coffee and breakfast.'

'I ordered it from your usual place,' she answered cryptically.

'I didn't know I had a usual breakfast place that also has a delivery service.' I almost always ate breakfast at the diner where Erica worked and they didn't deliver.

She responded by simply walking out of the room. A few seconds later, I heard her typing away at her desk.

I tested the coffee – warm but cool enough to drink – and demolished the bagel. After the two minutes that constituted my breakfast, I grabbed a seat on the corner of Pam's desk.

'Before I dozed off last night, I had a thought about how to nail Cooper.'

She stopped typing and looked up at me. 'Frame Ms Voss for something unrelated to blackmail, but related to financial fraud, like embezzling from HTS, and link it to her boyfriend and his room-mate?'

'Umm... yeah. That's exactly what I had in mind. How did you know?'

'You talk in your sleep.'

'I do?'

She shook her head no. 'Out of the several scenarios we could employ to fulfil the terms of our agreement with Mr Porter, having her steal from the company made the most sense. The manipulation of data to create a viable, but false, trail of theft played to our collective strengths. And it gives us some flexibility in terms of *how* we fulfil the terms of agreement with Mr Porter. I, also, anticipated your enjoyment of the irony.'

Damn her! She had taken the steam out of my big reveal. 'It does have a certain amount of elegance, doesn't it?'

'Yes, sir. They are attempting to steal from the company. We will simply change the terms to something they did not anticipate.'

'Alright. We have about a day to sort this out and execute a plan.'

'No, sir. We do not.'

'What do you mean?'

'The blackmailers sent Mr Porter another message moving the deadline to 6pm today. I believe it had something to do with your visit to his office yesterday. This also provides anecdotal evidence of Ms Voss's involvement. I do not doubt she informed Mr Cooper and Mr Dwerry of your visit.'

'Damn. We don't have much time to set this up.' I slid off her desk, intending to dash back to my office and get to work.

As usual, Pam stopped me. 'After I decided embezzlement was the best course of action, I took steps to implement the plan. That the deadline has changed should have no effect on its execution.'

I resumed my perch on her desk and rolled my wrist in the universal gesture to 'carry on'.

And she did. 'While you slept, I researched more into HTS and discovered their mining operation is a subsidiary company, headquartered on Kepler 62f. Fortunately, their financial division is located on Earth, which made manipulating their system easier.'

'So, you snuck in and are ready to transfer funds into an account owned by Ms Voss?'

Pam nodded. 'I've created an entire false trail of field survey requisition reports over the last eighteen months by a dummy corporation in Cooper and Dwerry's name.'

'How do you know Dwerry is involved?'

'A hunch.'

'A hunch? You have those?'

She ignored my question. 'Voss is the originator of the service request. Payments go to an account in a Singapore bank created in that company's name.'

'What did you name his company?'

'Does it matter?'

'Humour me.'

'Triumvirate Research and Operational Logistics, Ltd.'

I pondered the oddness of Pam's false company name and then it hit me. 'Wait, TROLL?'

She nodded. I laughed.

'All things considered, sir, it seemed appropriate.'

'Genius, Pam. Sheer genius. And let me guess, from this Singapore bank account, the money is siphoned into accounts owned by Cooper and Dwerry?'

'And Ms Voss.'

'What's left then? Break into their network and get ready to dump this on their system?'

'I completed that task as well.'

I nearly fell off her desk. 'You did all of this while I was asleep?'

'Though I am not the latest synthetic model, I can do more than answer phones and type reports.'

My mind raced through the plan. It was a good one, that's for sure. 'Sounds like you've thought of everyth—' The ring of the phone cut me off. Pam answered.

'It's Mr Porter.'

'Put him on speaker.'

I barely got 'hello' out before my client launched into a panic-filled diatribe. As soon as I explained to him we had a strategy in place – and that it was ready to go – he went quiet. Not unlike when Pam had taken the wind out of my sails a few minutes ago.

'I'll swing by your office later today,' I told him.

'Very good then.' Uncertainty dripped from his tone but he hung up all the same.

I looked back at Pam. 'So, I go over to Cooper and Dwerry's, bash the living hell out of them. While I'm doing that, you dump the embezzlement racket on their system.'

'Violence seems unnecessary to me. Can't we just execute my scheme and notify the police? Your direct involvement will drag us into any investigation that follows.'

'We could, but where's the fun in that? Besides they can't undo any of our handiwork if they're unconscious. And, if – or when – we get caught in the investigation, you better make sure it can't be traced back to us. You *are* that good, aren't you, Pam?'

She answered with a look of sheer venom. 'I am very good at what I do,' she replied in an injured tone. It was hard to believe she wasn't an actual human.

I slipped off her desk with a smile on my face and a spring in my step.

This should be fun.

Before I left the office, I grabbed two pairs of handcuffs, which I happened to possess legally; as well as a military grade stun gun, which I illegally possessed. The NEEDLE fired a single projectile in your choice of a neurological inhibitor for us fleshies or an EMP round that could take down your average robot.

I stuffed the bracelets and the gun, an extra tranquilliser round and a pair of leather gloves into a satchel, grabbed the laptop and went to chat with my office assistant one last time.

I slid the earpiece linked to my MAX into my ear. 'Once I have Cooper and Dwerry down, I'll give you the signal.'

'Very well, sir. Are you going straight there?'

'Not straight there, no. I thought it best to go home and change into something more appropriate.'

'Appropriate for what?'

'A pizza delivery guy.'

'I am sorry, sir, but I do not understand.'

'A disguise, Pam. I'll go to their building masquerading as a pizza delivery guy.'

'But you have no pizza.'

'I'll pick one up on the way.'

'Naturally, ahem, I – I should have assumed that.'

I walked out of my apartment building dressed like every guy who'd ever brought a pizza to my doorstep: jeans, T-shirt and a pair of generic loafers. I secured the stun gun in a shoulder holster and wore a khaki fatigue jacket to cover it.

On my way to the nearest subway station, I scrolled through Res 3's pizzeria choices and found one near Cooper's address. I ordered a basic ham and mushroom pie over the phone before descending into the bowels of the city's Underground network. One line-change and 15 minutes later, I paid for the pizza and hoofed it towards Berkshire Street.

The food smelled delicious and it got my stomach growling before I reached the end of the block. I figured I might as well stop for a minute to have a slice or two. It was nothing more than a prop after all. No reason to waste a perfectly good pizza. In the few seconds it took me to grab a wedge of cheesy goodness and lift it to my mouth, a man in a flat cap, black bomber jacket and aviators appeared on the other side of street and down the block from me.

I froze. With the pizza so close to my mouth, I couldn't resist taking a bite and tried to play it off as cool. I snuck a couple of peeks as I wolfed down the slice. It might have been the same guy who had tailed me, or it might not. No way to be certain at that distance. I could walk his way, maybe even break out into a sprint. However, with the head start he'd have, I doubted I could catch him.

I spoke in a low tone. The mic in the earpiece could pick up anything above the faintest of whispers. 'Pam, can you tap into the street cameras at my position? I think the guy who tailed me in the Electroglide yesterday is about a block east of where I'm standing.'

'Accessing them now. Are you eating something?'

I grabbed another slice and continued on my way at a slow, casual pace. 'Yeah, it's the pizza I bought as a cover.'

As soon as I started to move, the man in the flat cap turned and dashed around the corner. 'He's on the run. Do you have anything?'

'No, sir. His hat and sunglasses obscure too many of his features from the cameras. However, it appears he's walking towards the nearest subway station. Shall I continue to follow him?'

'Yes. But I'm already at 314 Berkshire and may also need your help getting in.'

'Will you require me to bypass the security measures on the main door?'

'Probably, but let me try to sneak in first.'

The building looked exactly like every other apartment building in the area – average, roughly cubic in shape and obvious signs of neglect. I scrolled through the directory until I found apartment D.

The 'genius' of my plan relied on someone coming out of the building right as I reached the entrance and I could just slip right in. But after a few minutes of waiting, I went to my second option.

'Okay, do your thing, Pam.'

'I assume you mean unlock the door?'

'Of course I do.' I sighed. Androids can be so literal sometimes – or all of the time.

The door clicked open and I slipped inside.

The interior of 314 Berkshire didn't look like the post-apocalyptic nightmare I envisioned. Some of the hovels in Residential 3 can be downright scary. However, this one had swept floors, walls devoid of graffiti or stains of any kind, and smelled of disinfectant. With pizza in hand, I rode the elevator to the fourth floor.

7

I stepped into a small communal area with four faded doors – all in need of a fresh coat of paint. Two faced the elevator. The other two flanked my left and right. The numbering scheme for this building made absolutely no sense. Before me were Cooper and Dwerry's apartment. Apartment Q, H and J completed the suite. The locations of apartments E, F or G – or even C for that matter – were anyone's guess.

'Okay, Pam. Showtime.'

'I do not fully understand the reference but I am ready nevertheless.'

'Good girl.'

I went up to the door labelled 'D' and knocked.

'Who's there?' came a muted reply as the volume cut on a video game or a movie; I couldn't really tell.

I stared at the digital peephole on the door so they could get a good look at me. 'I got a pizza here for Dwerry.'

'Pizza? I didn't order no pizza!' I heard from a different voice.

'Well, I have a pie with your name and address on it. Luther Dwerry, 314D Berkshire.' I held the box up to the small camera so they could see the name of the pizzeria: Buddy's.

'Why didn't you buzz us at the front door? How did you get in?'

'The intercom's busted and another tenant let me in.'

'Who?'

'I need a name,' I mumbled under my breath to Pam.

'Alfonso Dietrich. Aged sixty-eight. Lives in Apartment K on the second floor.'

'An old guy. Dietrich, I think he said his name was,' I said aloud. 'Look do you want the pizza or not? It's getting cold and my boss'll have my ass if I stroll back into work still carryin' the box.'

I heard the lock click and I reached under my jacket for the NEE-DLE's grip. As soon as the door opened wide enough for me to make out an entire torso, I brought the pistol out and fired all in one fluid motion. The shot hit a skinny, pale, blond guy with a puzzle beard square in the chest.

This was no sci-fi programme where I could set my phaser to stun and fire away like mad. I only had one shot, and I made it count. My target, Cooper it turned out to be, immediately started to go slack as the neurological inhibitor released into his body. I tossed the pizza box aside and bum-rushed my way into a jumbled mess of clothes, computer gear, monitors, video game systems and miscellaneous other crap. The place definitely lacked a woman's touch.

Cooper went down in a heap over a table covered with dirty plates, empty energy drink cans and console controllers. The momentum nearly took me with him. I managed to maintain my balance, which was a good thing, but lost the NEEDLE in the process.

My entrance had surprised and confused his roommate, who happened to be standing near a server cabinet. However, the guy recovered quickly and came at me from my right.

Luther Dwerry checked in around 185 centimetres and perhaps a shade over 100 kilos. He wasn't chiselled like Adonis or anything, but he didn't appear to be a slouch either.

He led with a serious right jab. I managed to dodge, and pivoted behind him as he followed through. I countered with a palm strike to the back of his head that sent him staggering into a metal shelving unit full of electronic crap.

'Start the transfer, Pam,' I said aloud.

'Who are you talking to?' Luther asked as he spun around, his right hand tucked behind his body. At that moment, the monitors in the room lit up with a whir of flashing financial statements and bogus websites.

'What the…? What the hell is going on here?'

'I don't know what you're talking about, Luther.'

'Bullshit!' he spat at me, and lunged again.

A glint of metal reflected in the light as a wicked-looking knife in his right hand slashed forward in a wide, mostly horizontal arc. Dwerry had the muscle. He had the mass. He just didn't have a lot of speed. I stepped diagonally into the attack, caught his wrist, and led with a right cross to his chin. The blow connected and carried through, allowing me to grab his shoulder. I forced him down as my right knee went up into his gut. The first one stunned him. The second one knocked the wind, and the fight, out of him. He dropped the knife on number three.

I twisted his arm behind his back and wrestled him to the ground in the next heartbeat. With his hand turned up at an awkward angle and me sitting on him like a school bully, Luther lay face down, groaning in pain. With my free hand, I grabbed a mass of hair and pulled it back.

'Who the fuck are you?' he asked through laboured breaths and blood-soaked spittle.

'Just a guy trying to earn a living.'

At this point I noticed a tear in my jacket surrounded by a blood-red stain. Even with my level of hand-to-hand combat training, it's difficult to engage someone with a knife and not take at least one hit. Knowing that didn't make me less pissed. I bounced his head off the floor.

'Ahhh! Fuck man! Listen,' he gasped. 'My friend and I... are... expecting a big payout—'

I leaned in. 'What's that?'

'Payout,' he said a little louder with effort. 'We can... give... you a cut... if... you let us... go.'

'Payout? And me a cut of the action?'

Dwerry nodded.

'I know all about it, Luther. Why do you think I showed up at your doorstep only hours before the deadline?'

And with that, I let go of his hand to free up my right and jacked him hard once in the temple. His head snapped left. His brain rattled off the side of his skull and he went lights out. I cuffed him and rolled him over into a recovery position.

With Dwerry secured, I checked on his partner in crime: unconscious but still breathing. I slapped a pair of bracelets on Cooper as well, and propped him against the couch.

'Situation under control, here, Pam. How are things on your end?' I asked as I took off my jacket to inspect the damage. Since he didn't possess a lot of skill with a blade, the cut wasn't deep. I doubted I needed stitches but I couldn't just leave it alone.

'Everything has been completed according to your instructions.'

'Did you find and delete the information pertaining to the Porter case?'

'All data was located and scrubbed from their hard drives.'

'And you checked any cloud servers that they could have used.'

'Naturally.'

'Any luck with the guy on the street?'

'No, sir. He is very skilled at shielding his features from the cameras.'

'Damn! Well, you did all that you could.'

I slipped on a pair of gloves and went over to a few monitors. Without any prompting, a few of them swapped to video game feeds and other streaming content. Only two of them displayed incriminating financial data.

'Are you doing this, Pam?'

'Yes, sir. I thought it would present a much more believable scene for when the police arrive.'

'Speaking of, I'll phone Ashdown.'

With Cooper and Dwerry dancing the cha-cha-cha with Mr Sandman, I placed a call to Metro HQ. A few seconds later, the switchboard put me through to a detective I'd worked with in another lifetime.

'Ashdown,' the voice announced over the phone.

'Hi, John. It's Daniel Helmqvist.'

'Oh, hey Dan. Been a long time. How's things?'

'Not too bad, thanks. Look, I've got a couple of guys tied up. You might want to send a few of New London's finest over here to check it out.'

'What the hell does that mean? No, no, don't answer that. I'm on my way,' he said with a mix of curiosity and suspicion. He knew I was a PI and I can only imagine what he thought I might be mixed up in.

'Oh, joy of joys. It'll be good to see you again, detective.'

'Just give me the address.'

'314 Berkshire, Res 3. Apartment D. Names on the registry are Alvin Cooper and Luther Dwerry.'

'Great. See you soon,' he said, before hanging up on me.

Ashdown and two uniforms came through the door of Cooper and Dwerry's place about 10 minutes after I had talked to him. He stood a bit taller than me and kept himself in decent shape for a guy pushing 60. Ashdown looked like he could hold his own in a fight. He shaved his head to hide his receding hairline. A pencil-thin beard hugged his jawline and chin like it was a fashion accessory.

The detective inspected the scene. His gaze moved from the two lowlifes I had tied up, around the room and then back to them. 'Now, what's this all about?'

'A job I'm working on led me to this address.'

'You're gonna need to give me more than that.'

I hemmed. He glared. Normally, I wouldn't divulge the identity of a client, but this was all going to be a police matter from here on out.

'The CEO of HTS Intergalactic suspected one of his employees was stealing from the company. The culprit turned out to be his assistant. A Ms Lyric Voss.'

'His assistant? Seems a bit clichéd doesn't it?'

'I thought the same thing. Turned out to be true and that these two upstanding gentlemen were in on the plot.'

'How do they figure into it?'

'The one with the peach fuzz on his cheeks is her boyfriend.' I pointed to one of the monitors with the planted evidence. 'Based on what I can tell, Voss created bogus invoices for an account in Singapore. HTS paid over three million credits to this account in the last year and a half. They split the money three ways into three more accounts, which made monthly deposits into the Martian bank accounts.'

'A million plus each?'

I nodded.

He looked around. 'They certainly aren't living the good life.'

I shrugged. 'A lot of gear in here and, who knows, maybe they were saving for retirement.'

Ashdown's gaze drifted to the floor and my NEEDLE.

'Let me get this straight. You paid those two a visit and it turned violent?'

I knew what was coming and tried to play it as cool as possible. 'Prospect of jail time will make people do all sorts of things.'

'Give me the details. Including why an illegal firearm is lying on the floor and one of the perps – Cooper, is it? – has a dart in his chest.'

'Carry-over from my services days. I forgot to hand it in on discharge and no one asked for it. I've held on to it ever since. Figured it might come in handy.' In truth, I had purchased it from a seedy contact. The detective didn't need to know that. 'Anyway, I entered their apartment to confront them about the embezzlement and things turned ugly. Cooper took a round in the chest. The other, Luther Dwerry, came at me with a combat knife. He even nicked me.' I showed Ashdown the cut. 'I defended myself. He got KO'd in the process. The jewellery on their wrists is mine.'

The detective processed my side of the story. 'With you, Helm, I doubt anything is that straightforward—'

'Why would I make this up?' He raised his hand to stop me.

'And I should haul your ass in on a possession of illegal firearms charge. But I'll let it slide this time since you didn't try to hide it. I'll get forensics in here to bag all their hardware. And you said the third person involved was an employee of HTS?'

'Lyric Voss.'

'Great. I may have more questions. Stay where I can find you.'

His last comments oozed sarcasm but I kept my trap shut. So far, I had survived this farce of my own doing. Without waiting for a reply,

Ashdown barked at the two uniformed cops on the scene to collar Dwerry and Cooper.

Immediately, the uniforms strapped levitation harnesses on the two poor saps and powered up the units with small remotes. The blackmailers would find out soon enough they were facing charges of stealing from HTS, but not for extortion. Their feet dangled about 10 centimetres off the ground. The officers piloted them out of the apartment like remote controlled ghosts.

As I grabbed the elevator before the officers could join me, I wondered if Alvin and the two other chipmunks would appreciate the irony.

On my way down to the ground floor, I called a taxi. It arrived at about the same time as the forensic unit. In they went and, as I watched them pass by me, I secretly hoped my set-up job would hold. Pam held up her end of the bargain beautifully and I had done mine well enough, I supposed.

During the taxi ride to HTS, I called Pam and told her to monitor Voss's phone and, also, to scan her computer for any more damning videos or evidence related to the case. Porter probably could have done this on his end, but I wanted to control the situation as much as possible.

She went to work immediately.

For my part, I rang Porter and told him there had been a break in the case and I was on my way over to see him. He and I had some colluding to do before Ashdown paid his assistant a visit.

8

No waiting around in the lobby this time. Porter greeted me almost as soon as I stepped through the main entrance.

'Mr Helmqvist, delighted to see you!' he said in his best Bertie Wooster.

'Is there some place private that we can speak? Preferably not your office?'

'Perhaps there is a free conference room,' he answered, taken aback by my enigmatic response. 'Allow me to confer with the receptionist.'

We walked over to the giant desk and he conferred away.

A few seconds later, he looked up at me. 'The second floor conference room is available. Would you like to follow me there?'

I nodded and followed.

'What is this all about?' he asked as soon as the elevator doors closed.

'Not here, Porter,' I replied without looking at him.

Behind the security of a locked conference room door, I cycled through the apps on my MAX smartwatch until I found a noise generator of my own design. Once I felt confident in our privacy, I told him everything that had happened since our last meeting.

His voice strained to contain his indignation. 'My assistant, Lyric, was a part of this whole scheme?'

'Unfortunately,' I answered, fighting back a chuckle. 'That's why I didn't want to meet you in your office. The moment she saw me, she'd know something was up.'

'Dreadful! I can scarcely believe it is true.'

'I had to give the police her name. They should be here any minute to take her in for questioning.'

'You are certain she will not confess to blackmail?'

I shrugged, palms upturned. 'She might. She can say whatever she wants, but the cops tend to follow the trail of evidence, which all points rather convincingly to her embezzling from you.'

'And all traces of the blackmail have disappeared?'

'They have. My office assistant is very thorough, if nothing else. However, while we are on the subject of the blackmail, I may have been too clever for my own good.'

'What do you mean?'

'As you now know, the funds being stolen came out of your mining subsidiary. I thought it would be ironic to burn them with the same division that they were using by way of that video to extort twenty million from you. However, the coming investigation might reveal your outfit on Ithilles.'

Porter waved his hand like a bored Caesar. 'We have been investigated several times. Without something like video evidence, the layers of subterfuge surrounding that particular mining operation are many, varied and difficult to penetrate. I doubt the police, or either legal team, will find anything untoward this time around.'

Wow! This guy was a piece of work.

'Wonderful. I'm just saying that you, and this company, will get dragged into the inquiry and the trial – if there is one. Be prepared. When they sit you down in the sweatbox, Metro will throw all kinds of theories at you—'

'Sweatbox?'

'Oh sorry... interrogation room. But yeah, all kinds of theories. If they are good, and Detective Ashdown is, they'll bring up your hidden planet and ask you if you committed genocide for economic gain.'

He shifted to the edge of his seat. Panic filled his eyes and his casual tone vanished in an instance. 'But you said the film has been destroyed!'

'Doesn't mean Voss, Cooper or Dwerry won't tell their side of the story. They will probably try anything to get a reduced charge. Again, though, it comes down to what can be proven. Want my advice?'

He nodded.

'Take a lawyer. The police will try to tell you guilty people hide behind a mouthpiece but don't take the bait. If you can, speak with him, or her, or them as soon as possible. Get your story straight and rehearse it.'

'That isn't much advice, Mr Helmqvist. I would never visit the police during an investigation without a lawyer present.'

'True. Here's the advice part: you do all the talking. Make it seem like your attorney is there for consultation purposes only. If they think you have nothing to hide, it might buy you some credibility.'

'Rather risky, don't you think?'

'It is, but this is also about selling the lie with conviction because they will check. They will verify everything you say and if anything is out of line the wheels'll come off this thing pretty quickly.'

'Anything else?'

'Yeah. When I come up in the conversation, drop the DA's name and that he referred me. Also, maybe have your lawyer remind them that our working relationship is confidential. That should end that line of questioning. Pissing the DA off has a way to ruin careers.'

'Is that all?'

I stood. 'Yep.'

He followed suit. 'Should I pay you now, then?'

'Let's wait until we see how this thing plays out. Once we know the three blackmailers are being charged for embezzlement, we can settle up.'

'Very good, Mr Helmqvist. We shall be in touch.'

'One more thing,' I called back as I made my exit. 'Sorry about taking three million and change without asking. I'm sure it'll be returned to you in the coming weeks.'

He chuckled lightly. 'I'm certain HTS will find a way to soldier on.'

Must be nice…

The cab ride back to the office gave me time to shift gears from my encounters with Cooper, Dwerry, Ashdown and Porter to the Rennick case. As the LTI pulled to a stop outside my building, I knew what I needed to do.

'Pam,' I announced as I marched through the front door. 'You beautiful woman, you! Why, under different circumstances I could kiss you right now!'

She stopped typing and looked up at me with her expressionless eyes. Definitely not inviting me to act out on any impulsive affection I may have been entertaining. Instead, I filled her in on what happened at 314D and my meeting with Porter in the aftermath.

'We should be looking at about twenty grand in a week or so. Not bad for a few days' work, eh?'

'Commendable, sir. And the Rennick case?'

Never messes around, this one. 'About that. I think I need to start my search at the heart of Kitterman's empire.'

'MARA Corporation?'

'Yep. I figure if she *is* holding onto a datapad that implicates her in mass murder, she'll keep it close by at all times.'

'If we disregard the illogic of maintaining the storage device in her possession, wouldn't it make more sense to hide it some place safer, such as her house or a bank deposit box?'

'I did consider those as options, and it may turn out that you're right, but I think her office is the place to start. MARA Corporation is her baby. It is, in a way, an extension of herself.'

A few years before Mara Kitterman's father died, she left Earth and relocated here, on Mars. She brought with her a ton of money and even more smarts. At the time, the scientific community was baffled as to why one of the great minds of our generation would leave the centre of civilisation and move to a colony that had little impact on the galactic scene.

Mara never provided an explanation. What she did do, though, was inject all of her resources into bolstering New London's university, funding civic improvements and starting her own company, Mars Advanced Robotics and Androids Corporation. Within five years, this dusty little rock floating around the Sun began to matter. Other companies, such as HTS, followed suit, and New London experienced a population boom of sorts. Not every district benefited from the boom equally, but life is rarely that generous.

'I concede your point, sir. Breaking into her office is a logical place to start.' *Did she just humour me?* 'How shall you accomplish this?'

I placed Rennick's business card on her desk. 'I'm glad you asked. I need you to call this number on a secure line and patch her back to me.'

Pam reached for her phone and I jumped in. 'Give me a minute or two first, alright?'

Her hand retracted silently and rested at the base of her keyboard. I dashed back to my office, fixed myself a gin and tonic in the previous night's filthy highball and settled into my chair. I had enough time for one pull on the glass before Pam announced Ms Rennick was on the line.

'Before you put her through, try to clone her phone during the conversation.'

'Yes, sir.'

A beep followed and I picked up.

'I didn't expect to hear from you so soon.'

'What can I say? I'm a fast worker.'

'So, you have something already?'

'More like I need something.' I took the silence on the other end as a cue to continue. 'Can you get me blueprints and schematic drawings of MARA Corp HQ? I'd like to follow up on some leads but I need access to her office.'

'Offices.'

'What?'

'She has two. One on the top floor of the executive building and one in R&D.'

'Damn. I can't go snooping around the entire complex. I'll be risking my neck just to get into the place. Any suggestions?'

'If you're after what I think you're after, I would search the executive building. There are far too many employees with access to her office in R&D for it to be considered a secure location. Whereas her other one is only used when she's in there. It's more like a sanctuary to her.'

Sanctuary, bingo!

'Sounds like the place to start looking. Can you get me the prints?'

'I can.'

'Excellent. Meet me at DKY tomorrow at 8.30pm.'

'Seems like a rather public place for an exchange of this nature, Mr Helmqvist. Is there some place else we could do this?'

'I'll be there on a date. I can pop over to the bar to meet you and then slip back to my table. It'll make for a nice cover and we should be able to hide in the crowd. Trust me, it's the perfect place.'

Her *okay* did not brim over with confidence. However, she agreed and terminated the call.

Without a sound, Pam appeared in my doorway but said nothing.

'Were you able to access her phone?'

'No, sir. I required more time to break through her encryption protocols.'

'Ah well, you tried. I'd be worried if it was so easy to clone her phone.'

'Perhaps…' And her voice trailed off.

I drained my glass, grabbed a small, black box from the centre drawer in my desk, checked the contents – a pair of simple, gold earrings – and stood to make my exit.

'Time to call it quits for today, I think. I'm off to 3rd Street to unwind. If anyone calls wanting to discuss a case, take a message this time and leave me be.' I punctuated my demands with a wink.

In response, Pam went back to her desk and began typing away at her furious, determined pace.

9

The next day, a phone call from Detective Ashdown ruined my plans to chill out until my date with Erica. He requested my presence down at Metro HQ for some questions. From his tone, I knew I had two options: say 'you got it' and get to Research District 1 as quickly as possible, or say 'no' and get hauled in by some beat cops. Needless to say, five minutes after hanging up with the detective, I sped towards the central dome in the back seat of a black LTI.

Thirty minutes later, I slouched in a hard metal chair of a fourth-floor interrogation room, staring at my reflection and trying not to think about the cameras trained on me from their hovering positions at the corners of the ceiling to my left and right. Eventually, Ashdown joined me.

'How's your arm?'

I pulled my sleeve up to show a bandage wound tight around my forearm. 'Good, thanks.'

Pleasantries out of the way, he jumped right in. 'You stated the purpose of your visit to 314D Berkshire was because of an investigation into the illicit activities of an HTS employee. Is that correct?'

'That's right. Didn't your tech crew find anything?'

The detective glanced down at his MIX11, made a swiping motion and then back to me. 'Yeah, they found exactly what you told me they would find. And I mean *exactly*.'

I shrugged. 'I did my homework before I made a move on them. It's exact because that's what happened.'

'Cooper, Dwerry and Voss are telling a different story.'

'Ah, for fuck's sake—'

'Hey! Watch the language in here, pal!'

'Fine! For Christ's sake, Ash. Is that better?'

He glowered. I continued, 'Like a perp's never told a lie during an interrogation. Dangle some pie-in-the-sky story and hope you bite on it.'

'So, you didn't enter their building disguised as a pizza delivery guy and attack Cooper and Dwerry without provocation?' He left out the NEEDLE, which I thought was a nice gesture, but it didn't give him a free pass.

'Cooper, Dwerry *and* Voss said I did this? Voss, who was working during the incident?' I can cross-examine, too.

The detective glanced down at his tablet again in frustration. 'No. Cooper and Dwerry told that one. Those two plus the girlfriend have confessed to attempted blackmail. They had no idea about the bank accounts and seemed genuinely surprised to learn they were already millionaires.'

'Blackmail is less time, right?'

'Yeah.'

'Imagine that. Confessing to a lesser charge. Feigning surprise at the hidden money. Is there no limit to the level of deviousness these three possess?'

'Can it, Helm! The thing is, they are all telling the same story. How HTS discovered a planet, didn't tell anyone about it and wiped out a species to gain access to raw materials.'

'And you believe them? Have you found anything to support these allegations?'

'Not really and no. But through isolated interviews the level of detail they've given is precise and consistent.'

'Maybe they rehearsed a scenario like this. Draw out the investigation and buy for more time.'

'Maybe.'

'Anyway, what does it matter? You've got what you need on them, right?'

'We do.'

'Then what's this all about?'

'You don't have a monopoly on being thorough, Helm.'

'Superb! Can I go now?'

He spun his MIX11 around, facing me. 'Review this statement. If it jives with your account of what you've told Metro PD, sign it and you can go back to enjoying your Saturday.'

Everything looked to be on the up and up, so I scrawled my signature.

The detective and I parted ways at the on-duty desk. 'Remember, until this thing is closed, don't go anywhere.'

'I guess I'll have to cancel my climbing trip up Mount Alba. Which is a pity because I've heard it's lovely in the spring. Flowers coming into bloom. Trees lush and green. But if you insist…'

Ashdown shook his head and walked away.

On the way back to my apartment, I called Pam to let her know about my interview and reflected on how much trouble I'd be in if Porter's nasty little secret came to light. I shuddered and quickly moved on to other worries.

Several hours later, I walked out of my apartment, dressed in a dark grey wool three-piece with a white shirt and champagne-coloured silk tie. I don't wear that tie too often but I figured I should make an effort to liven up my ensemble. On my way to my car, I double-checked my inside breast pocket to make sure the cheap pair of gold earrings I had taken from my office yesterday hadn't disappeared under mysterious circumstances. An app I had installed on my MAX confirmed that the tracking device in the earrings worked, as well. So far, so good.

On my way to Erica's, I called Steve and asked if he could pick me up outside my house tonight at 2am. I was taking a helluva risk by dragging him into my scheme but I needed a driver. At first, he hesitated to agree. Let's face it: people going out at that hour are rarely off to Mass. He came around, though, when I agreed to triple his fee and include a generous tip.

By 7.30, Erica and I cruised through her neighbourhood, Residential 2, towards the Financial District. Skalpel's *Polish Jazz* played in the background. Erica looked like a knock-out.

Over a sheath-style dress as dark as night, which stopped at mid-thigh, she wore a black, sheer maxi-dress. A stitched floral pattern trailed down both sleeves and the main body of the fabric. A pair of matching sandals with leather straps and a bit of a heel to them completed the ensemble. Her straight, dark hair fell to her shoulders with a single, long braid on the right side tucked behind her ear. She had applied her make-up with artful skill.

'I didn't know you had a car, Danny?' she asked as we cruised through the high-end dome, Residential 1.

'Yeah, I only bring it out on special occasions.' This was partially true. Parking in New London cost a fortune so I tended to only drive to places where it didn't cost a day's salary to leave it – namely, my apartment, my office or 3rd Street. Anyway, the comment won me some points.

'I've never seen one like this before. Is it new?'

'The Griffon is about five years old. Nash only ever made a handful of them as prototypes.' The car had a wide stance and more curves than a burlesque dancer. It looked like something out of the 1930s. Its simulated exhaust gave the normally lifeless whir of the electric motor a deep, throaty growl.

'And you got one?'

'Payment on a case.'

'Really? You must be one tough negotiator.'

'I guess it depends on how much I like my clients.'

'And what about me? What if I was one of your clients?'

'I'll just say, I'm glad you aren't running Nash or we'd be in a cab right now.'

The Financial District loomed in the distance. I had just enough time to spring my meeting with Rennick on Erica before we rolled up to DKY's valet parking stand. All things considered, she took it well, but then again she seemed fairly easy-going.

DKY billed itself as Pacific Rim and jazzed the place up with a decor somewhere between the ancient and the modern. A minimalist electronic interpretation of traditional Japanese music played in the background; simple melodies played on *kotos* and bamboo flutes woven together with a nice selection of down-tempo backbeats and loops.

The maître d', and my sometimes drinking partner when I'm not slumming in the IM, Dominic set us up at a cosy table for two in an out of the way spot. I kicked the night off with a reliable gin and tonic. Erica went for a chardonnay. Our conversation fell into a lull while we considered the options on the menu.

A waiter stalked up with perfect timing to take our orders. Erica chose the seared tuna with a ginger-miso sauce. It came with a julienned sweet potato and crispy sushi rice salad tossed in a wasabi oil dressing. I opted for a pork loin chop crusted with *panko* and *togarashi*. They served the breaded loin with grilled vegetables, lentils and a shallot soy-mustard sauce. For a starter, I picked a bowl of sweet chilli edamame and another with garlic sauce. To drink, Erica and I agreed on a bottle of *Junmai-shu*, chilled.

We toasted the evening and the banter went down as easy as the booze.

'Are you wearing one of your own creations?' I asked after a sly up and down of her perfect figure.

'I am. How did you guess?'

'Just lucky, I suppose.'

I said before that Erica worked at one of my local haunts, which was true. However, her ambition in life was to make it in the fashion industry. She and her roommate Chloe MacDonald met in UNL's design programme, have been friends since and have turned their two-bedroom apartment into a mini studio. Based on what she wore, I had no doubt she'd make it in the business sooner rather than later.

'Well, you don't look too bad yourself.'

I tilted my glass towards her in salute. 'Why thank you. I have the fortunate privilege of living above a tailor's shop. In fact, I should introduce you to him. I wouldn't be too surprised if Rick's got connections.'

'That's very sweet of you, Danny. It'd be great to meet him.'

The appearance of Dominic brought the conversation to an abrupt halt.

'Sorry to disturb you both, but I have a message for Mr Helmqvist.'

He handed me a folded piece of paper, and drifted back to his position near the entrance.

I examined the note:

I'm at the bar. C

'Right on time,' I said under my breath.

'What is it?' asked Erica.

'My client. She's here.'

I picked my way past other diners and found Charlotte Rennick sitting in a tiny booth tucked into the corner of the bar area. She toyed with a glass of wine in one hand and held a menu in the other.

She smiled politely when she saw me. I reciprocated and eased in next to her.

'You look very dapper tonight,' she said as she let the menu fall onto the table.

'Why thank you. You look pretty good yourself.'

She wore a fashionable sleeveless dress with a high neckline and the skirt bunched at the waist. I couldn't really tell because of the table and her posture but I assumed that the pleating gave a bit of a flared-look to it. The colour – a soft shade of coral – offset her complexion perfectly.

'It's nice to see you haven't lost your charm, Mr Helmqvist.'

Exchanging pleasantries wouldn't get me back to the table with Erica so I hurried the conversation along. 'Do you have what I asked for?'

'I do.'

Setting her wine goblet down, Charlotte reached into her purse, pulled out a portable storage device and placed it next to the menu. Without looking at it, I palmed it with my right hand and placed my left on top of it.

'Excellent. All the details?'

She nodded.

'Good. I'm going to go in there tonight and poke around.'

'What about your date?'

'*Late* tonight.'

'And starting at MARA Corp is the best first move?'

I shrugged. 'As good a place as any.'

'Perhaps you are right,' she said finally.

'One more thing, before I go. I have something for you.'

I reached into my breast pocket, which also gave me a chance to drop the storage device in there, and pulled out a small, plain black box. I handed it to her.

'What's this?'

'A present.'

'Really, you shouldn't have.'

'Go on. Open it.'

She tilted back the lid to reveal the simple-looking pair of gold earrings. She looked at me with slight confusion.

'I'm not joking. You *really* shouldn't have.'

'Do you like them?' I asked cryptically.

She looked at them again. 'They're nice, I guess.'

I laughed. I didn't need to be a PI to deduce her true opinion of those cheap-looking baubles resting on a tiny pillow.

'I'd like you to have these on at all times.' I took them out of the box and showed her the flat backings to them. 'See, you can even wear them while you're sleeping.'

'This is all very odd, Mr Helmqvist. Why would I wear these earrings all of the time? Or why should I even accept them? We hardly know each other.'

'They are a tracking device of my own creation. I'll be able to keep an eye on your location.'

'Perhaps I don't want you to know my every movement,' she replied business-like.

An image of the guy tailing me flashed before my eyes. 'You might not be safe after tonight, Charlotte, that's why… or you might be perfectly safe, I can't really say. All I know is I'll feel better if I can check in on your location from time to time.'

'You think I might be in danger?' The concern in her tone was real.

'Honestly, I do. If this thing is as big as you believe it to be then I think quite a few people's lives could be at stake. So will you wear them?'

She looked at the box suspiciously.

'I'm not sure. MARA Corp has a pretty advanced security system and it might detect the signal these things emit.'

'They work on a modulating frequency that'll piggy-back onto any wireless signal for only a short period of time before finding another. They will be very hard to detect.'

'And you trust that they work?' she said as she looked from the box to me.

'I designed them so of course I do.'

She glanced quickly at the earrings with renewed interest.

'You made these?'

'Mmmhhmm.'

'You're a man of many talents.'

'I guess I've picked up a few skills along the way.'

She started to remove her own earrings and put the others in. *Good girl*, I thought to myself.

'Care to elaborate?'

'Not right now, sorry.' I almost said 'Charlie' but I caught myself. Instead, I glanced at my watch; too much time had passed. 'Listen, I need to get back to my date. Thanks again for the information and for being so agreeable about the tracking devices.'

She dropped the case into her purse.

'I'll keep an eye out for anything unusual after tonight,' she said as she watched me get up. 'If there is any fallout after your visit to MARA Corp, I should know about it.'

'Excellent. Call me on Monday – any time of the day will be fine. We can arrange a meeting and discuss new developments.'

'Of course, Mr Helmqvist,' she replied quietly.

'Be careful, and I mean that.'

'You too.'

I made tracks back to my table and a waiting Erica.

The edamame and the sake had arrived. From what I could tell as I worked my way through the seating area, Erica looked bored. No one liked dining alone.

'I am really sorry about that, and I promise no more distractions tonight.'

'That's alright, Danny. I'm just glad that it didn't take too long.'

I grabbed the *tokkuri*, filling an empty *ochoko* almost to the brim with sake. I also refilled Erica's small ceramic cup.

'What do you think of the sake?'

'It's nice. It reminds me of a chardonnay that I like to keep around the apartment.'

'Perfect! It looks like I'm batting a thousand right now.' I held up my cup. 'To no more interruptions.'

She clinked hers to mine.

Neither of us took our eyes off the other as we both took a sip of our rice wine.

With its fruity aroma and slight hint of pear, I knew that I had made the right choice. The oak finish lingered a nice long while on my palate. I could drink this all night if I didn't have a felony to commit later on.

We didn't have too long before the waiter came to tell us that our main courses were coming out soon. I had had just enough time to sample both types of edamame and put my hunger in a momentary headlock.

Two hours later, we had demolished our main courses, moved on to our second bottle of sake and as much of our pasts as we dared to share. She told me about her family. She's first generation Martian. Her parents immigrated to the Red Planet to work in one of the agricultural domes as bioengineers. Her only sibling, an older brother, works at a research station on Titan. For my part, I told her how my grandfather came to Mars to work the mines in the rock cliffs outside the domes. I had no brothers or sisters and my father worked for the city power company as an electrical engineer. My mother died when

I was young. My father died when I was older. At present, I was the last Helmqvist on Mars.

At the end of dinner, while waiting for the valet to bring the car around, Erica expressed an earnest desire to see my apartment. I couldn't have hoped for a better progression of the evening.

10

The drive from the Financial District to my apartment passed in a blur. 'Music to Make Love to Your Old Lady By' flowed out of the car's speaker system like an extension of my thoughts. Erica had her head turned away from me, watching the world race by through the passenger window. Her left hand rested on my thigh a little higher than Mrs Grundy would've approved of. Anticipation hung as sweetly in the air as her perfume.

A dozen jack moves, a few close calls with speed cameras later, we had arrived outside my building. I didn't bother with parking the Griffon in its space in a nearby structure. Getting inside my apartment was far too compelling to worry about where to leave a car.

'Nice place you have here, Danny.' Erica made a quick survey of my pad as I took her wrap and hung it in the closet.

'Thanks. Feel free to make yourself at home.'

She settled herself on the couch in a way that could only be called beguiling. I checked the time on my **MAX** smartwatch. Still time before the caper and no clue as to what I was doing. I pulled up my apartment's hi-fi system on the wrist device and chose Monk's 1953 self-titled album in the belief it would inform my next moves.

The arrhythmic piano strokes of 'April in Paris' filled the room, and I dimmed the lights to add to the ambience.

'This is nice,' she announced when the music began.

'I'm happy to hear that. Can I get you something to drink?'

'Sure, Danny. Wha'cha got?'

'Well, I'm no mixologist but I know the classics.'

'Surprise me.'

I grabbed some simple syrup, and a couple of basil leaves, limes and cucumber slices from the refrigerated compartment of my mini bar and muddled them all together in a shaker. Some ice, a shot of gin, shake for 10 seconds, into a cocktail glass with a basil leaf for the finishing touch.

I went for a basic gin and tonic that was mostly tonic.

She reached for her drink and I plopped down next to her. We turned to face each other.

'Cheers.'

Erica clinked her glass against mine and we drank.

'That's pretty good! What is it?'

'A cucumber basil gimlet.'

'Gimlet? When you said you knew the classics, I didn't expect this. I feel like I'm in a Bogart movie. It's good though.'

'I'm glad to hear you like it.' Our conversation picked up but I couldn't shake the distraction of what was still to come.

'You live here alone?'

'I do.'

'It must cost a fortune.'

'The rent isn't too bad. I actually own the place.'

'You own this apartment?'

I nodded again.

'Are you loaded or something?'

I don't think that she would normally ask me a direct question like that. She didn't seem like the type, but hooch has a great way of lowering inhibitions.

'Remember when I said that I practised law once upon a time? I had a small nest-egg from that gig and some inheritance money.'

She finished her drink and sat the empty glass on the coffee table. We locked gazes. Her brown eyes stared into my soul. She knew my mind wasn't fully on the moment. And said as much.

'What's up, Danny? You seem…' She furrowed her brow. *My God was she beautiful.* '…distracted. You're definitely somewhere else right now and here I went through all this trouble to ensure your attentions stayed fully on me.'

I chuckled to buy a little time. The booze. The music. The girl. It was a perfect night. Better than most I'd ever had. Her hand dropped back to her lap.

In that moment, I took a leap of faith. I laid it all on the line and prayed that Erica liked me as much as I thought she did. As much as I liked her. If she didn't have the same level of feelings, sneaking into MARA Corporation would be a no go because I wouldn't risk it.

'Sorry. You're right. I have been distracted. It's just that I have something I need to do tonight—'

'And our date is getting in the way of that? Should I go?'

I put my hands on her knees. 'It's nothing like that…' And I drifted off in thought.

'What else?' Her tone was not accusatory; only curious.

After a deep breath, I continued. 'It isn't exactly legal. And, it isn't something I've ever attempted before – at least not on this scale.'

I could see the question coming, so I cut it off at the pass. 'I can't go into it. I can never discuss a case with anyone else.'

What came next was completely unexpected. 'Would an alibi help you with tonight?' A sly grin pulled at the corner of her lips.

'Umm… yeah. It would actually.'

'Then you have it.'

'Have what?'

'An alibi!'

Erica had me thoroughly confused now. 'What?'

She laughed. 'With this line of questioning, I can see why you gave up being a lawyer.'

I flushed with embarrassment. 'It was easier to focus in a court-room than on this couch with you.'

Erica leaned in and kissed me softly. 'I'll be your alibi for tonight.'

I moved from her lips to her neck and whispered into her ear. 'I can't ask you to do that. It's too dangerous. I think you know how much trouble you could get into if you lied to the cops, and they found out.'

'Danny, I've been waiting a long time for this night. I've been waiting and waiting for you to pluck up the courage to ask me out. I like you. I like you a lot. If me sticking to a story keeps you out of trouble so that we can do this again, I'm willing to risk it.' She began to nibble on my ear. 'Besides, I'm starting to find the idea of helping you on one of your jobs to be exciting.'

'How exciting?'

'Very. Just don't get caught tonight.' The sound of her voice and the warmth of her breath in my ear sent shivers down my spine.

My hands cradled the base of her head, fingers entwined in her hair, and our lips locked in clumsy passion. Each of her kisses carried with it a hint of basil. 'Just You and Me' had started playing. Things started to get hot and heavy.

Erica swung her right leg over mine and straddled me before I could process anything. Our fervour sped right past *hot* and *heavy* towards *unbridled* without so much as a howdeedoo. We stayed like this for an eternity wrapped in minutes. By the time 'Liza' came on, I decided a change of venue was in order and stood, cupping her ass to keep her close to me. She hooked her feet around my waist, and I carried her into the bedroom.

When I actually noticed the music again, 'Ruby, My Dear' wafted into the room. Monk had ended and another of his albums began to play. Erica lay beside me, asleep, breathing softly. I set my alarm on my MAX for half past midnight. I needed some sleep myself before I reviewed the information on the flash drive and Steve picked me up.

It couldn't have been more than a couple of seconds before my watch vibrated silently. I woke up and felt like shit. At least Erica looked perfectly content. In the dim glow of the streetlights, I couldn't get over that stunning beauty next to me; the sheets only partly covered her naked body.

As I crawled out of bed, I could hear the hi-fi system continuing through my collection of Monk. *Thelonious in Action* played softly in the living room and the track 'Evidence' had just come on.

How fitting.

I grabbed some clothes and ducked into the bathroom. A quick shower perked me up a bit. Once dressed, I went to the kitchen for water and aspirin, and slammed a vial of concentrated guarana. I fetched the storage device Rennick had given me earlier that night, closed the bedroom door and returned to the bathroom with my MIX12.

With 15 minutes to spare, I had the workings of a plan but it required some gear from my office: an easy enough detour en route to RD1. I stuffed the tablet into a satchel and stole a peek at Erica one last time.

She looked so peaceful.

Getting back into bed and waking next to her in the morning provided me with a powerful incentive to get in to MARA Corp, get what I need, and get out undetected.

Going out the bathroom window and down the fire escape might seem a little extreme when you're doing it from a place you own. But I couldn't risk a person, or a camera, spotting me as I strolled out the front door. Despite the near Big Brother levels of surveillance New London possessed with its cameras, alleyways rarely had any coverage. The city left it to the owners of the buildings to monitor what went on behind their establishments.

I kept to the shadows under a baseball hat and a pair of wayfarers as I watched a black LTI turn down the street. The car pulled up to the kerb slowly and came to a stop.

'Perfect timing,' I said as I hopped in.

'I aim to please, Mr Helmqvist.'

'Call me Dan.'

'Sure thing. Where to?'

'My office over on Tireman. Then, MARA Corp.'

'You got it, boss,' he said as we took off.

Not much life in the Commercial District during the small hours of night; a good time to be up to no good. Steve dropped me off at the end of the block and kept the engine running.

To avoid another set of street cameras and prying eyes, I kept my head down and my face out of view. I strolled past my office building, around the corner and into an alley where a back entrance glowed under a single, overhead lamp. The guy who owned it didn't bother with a camera; only a basic alarm system. I deactivated it with my MIX12 and crept up a set of service stairs to the second floor.

As soon as the front door of my office opened and I stepped into the reception room Pam emerged from a sidewall panel like a vampire coming out of her mausoleum.

'Goddammit, Pam! I nearly pissed myself!'

She glanced down at my crotch expecting to see a wet spot. 'My apologies, sir, but as you know, I am programmed to activate if the front door is opened when I am in my recharging station.'

'I *do* know. I'm a bit edgy at the moment and forgot about your protocols, that's all.' My heart rate slowed to normal. 'Anyway, I'm here to pick up a few things and then I'll be on my way.'

'Do you require assistance?'

'No… In fact, it would be good if you could scrub this from your memory banks. I need you to have no knowledge of my coming here.'

'Very well,' she said as she stepped back into her compartment. 'Please remember to lock up before you leave.' The wall panel door closed with a *swoosh* and a *thunk*.

In one corner of a conference room I had no particular use for stood a Mosler T2K nearly my height and twice my width. The safe came with a biometric scanner, keypad and mechanical tumbler that made it one of the tougher nuts to crack. Which was a good thing because it held a prized possession: an expensive and very illegal-to-own crime-fighting costume.

The full-body suit, a variation on the Martian Special Forces Enhanced Mobility Suit, Mark 9 design, consisted of matching headgear, a backpack and a belt with small storage compartments. All of it dyed a shade darker than up-to-no-good black. It had earned the nickname FE9 because we all like a good pun.

The suit's material allowed me to regulate the temperature signature that my body emitted to read at ambient; to an infrared sensor, I would be invisible. It also provided some protection against the harsh environment outside the domes. Shock-absorbing pads safeguarded the knees and elbows of those prone to falling.

The soles of the boots had an Electromagnetic Levitation system fitted to them; a feature essential for bypassing pressure sensitive pads. However, the EML installed in this model of boot lack a means of stabilisation, which makes keeping your balance difficult and takes practice. Some have compared the sensation of levitating while wearing these boots to a surfer catching a wave and staying up on his, or her, board. Pity we don't have any oceans on this dusty rock to test that theory.

The gloves could be used to duplicate finger and handprints – perfect for getting around some biometric systems. The thumb of the right glove also possessed a fake ID chip for all manner of bogus transactions.

The headpiece resembled a glorified balaclava made from the same material as the rest of the suit. The visor worked as an optical head-mounted display, providing environmental feedback and recording capabilities with a built-in digital camera. The visor also had the ability to serve as a monitor for the computer tucked away in the backpack, which took first prize in the cool factor in my humble estimation.

Made from a sturdy high-resin polymer, the pack kept all of the FE9's systems running, and me plugged into the city's virtual network. And, best of all, a built-in jump jet. That's right, a freaking jump jet capable of propelling the wearer to a maximum height of 40 metres in a 1g environment; much higher in lower gravity. A combination of hand movements in the gloves and a wireless connection to my watch-controlled thrust and direction.

I doubted that my decision to use it on Saturday night could be construed as smart, or even wise. I had never really done anything more than familiarise myself with the controls and respec the computer for a wide assortment of illicit activities. I had never used it in a live scenario either. In fact, I wouldn't have dared to use it for a break in to MARA Corporation if I felt like I had a better option. It was the suit, or nothing.

I stripped down to my skivvies and pulled it on. I synced up my MAX smartwatch and ran through a systems check. Everything passed and I had nothing left to do but sneak into one of the most advanced companies in the entire system.

I stuffed the gloves and the headgear into their allotted storage space in the backpack, slid my jeans and button-up shirt over the FE9 and grabbed my jacket on the way out. Looking at me, you would never know that I wore something straight out of the comic books underneath.

I retraced my steps out of the building, reset the alarm and found Steve waiting to go at the other end of the block.

11

Kitterman Drive, the main north–south street, ran straight through RD1, interrupted on only two different occasions: the roundabout in the very centre of the dome and **MARA** Corporation. The road picked back up on the other side of Kitterman's headquarters and continued to the Research District 2 connection tunnel. Four roads with equally uninspiring names – Corporations North, East, South and West – squared in the two buildings, which composed the core of her empire.

In the darkness, the roundabout glowed like a beacon under the intense beams of a dozen floodlights, signalling to the rest of the galaxy that New London mattered. All great metropolises have an enormous thoroughfare at their nexuses for all to marvel at. The intersection a block south of **MARA** Corp marked the convergence of the dome's four major avenues: Kitterman, Congress, Franklin and New Street. A statue of the Roman god Mars stood majestically on a huge marble base at the centre of the roundabout. The enormous monument loomed over 10 metres tall and the subject matter demonstrated a complete lack of originality.

Mars on Mars.

But tourists loved to crowd around it and snap photos like it was a celebrity. Late at night, however, the taciturn giant held his vigil without the benefit of an adoring crowd.

A large sash, in gold fabric to honour New London's approaching sesquicentennial, hung from his right shoulder down to his left hip like he was a contestant in a beauty pageant. Printed in black, block capitals on the front of the sash was the slogan: 'Celebrating 150 Years of Life on Mars'.

Like Porter said, this town began as nothing more than a research station and a launch pad. As it advanced in the field of human habitation and 1g technology, so did New London. The dome we currently drove through was the first to be constructed. Tunnels ran out from RD1 like spokes on a wheel. More domes were built and connected to one another. Slowly, my city took shape and is now home to over half a million people.

I asked Steve to drop me off at the corner of Franklin and Corporation South. A manhole located there led to one of the many service corridors between the world above and the world below.

This particular tunnel serviced a nearby Underground line and connected to another passageway, which ran conveniently close to MARA Corporation. It'd allow me to get as close as possible to my target destination without running the risk of being seen above ground. I didn't need videos of me in a super-suit jumping around New London popping up on the internet. It might blow my cover.

Steve glided through the roundabout onto Franklin and pulled the taxi over at the kerb. I put my right thumb up to the chip reader and paid him through a dummy account I had set up when I first became a PI.

'Don't leave just yet, Steve,' I said as I got out. He waited. I stepped around to his side of the car and he put the window down.

'Take this,' I said and handed him an earpiece. He looked at it suspiciously. 'You and I will be able to communicate through an open, encrypted channel.'

'I thought that I would just wait for you on Division. Are you sure this is safe?'

'We'll call this a change of plans and don't worry, it's safe. The signal will constantly cycle through multiple sources per second. It's very hard to trace.'

It sounded like a load of malarkey but Steve took the comm-unit anyway.

'It'll allow us to adapt to any emergencies that might arise,' I continued. An image of my body bouncing off the side of a building like a rag doll, jetpack firing uncontrollably, flashed through my mind.

'You got it, Mr Helmqvist.' He clipped the device onto his ear. It looked like a fairly ordinary hands-free unit.

'There is a small button that you press to turn it on.' I reached in and pressed it. 'Once it's on, you can talk freely, so mind what you say.'

He threw me a wink and drove away slowly. With my hat pulled tight over my eyes to avoid facial recognition, I watched him round the corner and disappear into the urban jungle. A few seconds later, I took off down the sidewalk in the direction of the service hatch. Before I reached my destination, I ducked down another narrow, dark alley between two large and impressive piles of steel and concrete.

I found a spot away from the ever-present street lamps and surveillance cameras. I took off my outer layer of clothing and immediately realised I didn't have any place to store them; only the gloves and malleable head gear fit in the compartmental spaces of the backpack.

I checked the pouches on the suit's belt and found an evidence bag that could easily hold my trousers, shirt, shoes, jacket and hat. I jammed them all in, sealed it and looked for a place to hide the pouch.

In the end, I decided that if a skip or booth worked in the comic books, one would work for me. A couple of promising candidates sat at the end of the alley. I wedged the bag behind one of them and hoped for the best. I slid on my helmet, secured the backpack, attached the air hose to the mouthpiece, tightened up the belt, powered up the FE9 and prowled off to my date with a tunnel.

The alley I had used for my quick change connected to a larger system. It allowed me to reach the first access hatch quietly and unnoticed.

I negotiated my way through this maze of narrow lanes as silent as a shadow. In the top left-hand corner of my UI, a small map helped guide me to my destination. En route, I thought it best to try out the comm-link with Steve. I switched on my earpiece and I could hear music playing in the background.

'Test. One. Two. Three.'

'Roger that,' Steve replied. The music stopped.

'Good, it's working,' I said as I crept along. 'Remember to keep it on the whole time.'

'You got it, Mr Helmqvist.' A pause and then he continued. 'You seem to have a lot going on for an average-looking guy. I mean you're a private investigator. You have this crazy suit and you're good with computers. What gives?'

'Average-looking? I'm hurt. I usually go for dashing.'

'Oh! I didn't mean your looks.'

'You been checking me out, Steve?'

'Maybe I shoulda used unassuming.'

'Well, tuxedos and martinis only work in the movies. I find it best to keep a low profile. You know, unassuming.' He couldn't see my grin.

The density of the ambient sound over his mic increased. He must have entered one of the tunnels connecting RD1 to another part of the city.

'Seriously, though, what's the story?'

'Well, let's just say that I'm an over-achiever... Wait. Hold on one second.'

'Roger,' he replied.

I liked that. It gave my little mission an air of authenticity.

I broke off the conversation because I had reached my next obstacle. To your average New Londoner, it looked like nothing more than your run-of-the-mill manhole cover. However, to those in the know, these portals granted entry into a subterranean byzantine world of intersecting and meandering tunnels.

My gateway to the very inner workings of the city itself.

Unfortunately, a central hub monitored these electronically locked hatches. The city didn't want just anyone prying one open and disappearing into its bowels. I could try to bypass the system but I would risk being spotted by a passer-by. In the end, I went for the simple and direct route.

I grabbed a silver disc, about the size and shape of a hockey puck, out of my belt. It gave off a powerful but contained burst of energy, which would disable any electrical device within an 18-metre radius.

I placed it next to the manhole, pressed a small button on the top and ran for it. I had 20 seconds to distance myself from the discharge radius or be caught in the blast, zapping the FE9's electronics. I'm not sure if the EMP would destroy the systems installed on it but I doubted it would do them any favours.

I legged it further down the alley and took up a position in a doorway far enough away from the cover. A few seconds later I saw a nearby streetlamp go out.

Success.

I had to move quickly. The power outage would have subway workers, and possibly the police, here in a few minutes.

It took me longer than I wanted, but eventually I managed to get the cover off and clambered down a set of metal rungs attached to the tunnel wall before anyone arrived at the scene. The lid clanged loudly as I slid it back into place; echoes bounced down the endless length of the pitch-black tunnel.

'Okay. I'm in,' I said over the comm-link.

'Nice one. What's it like in there?'

I switched on a small headlamp and scanned up and down the corridor.

'It's dark,' I whispered, but in the quiet and empty space of the tunnel I might as well have been yelling at the top of my lungs. 'And the air is warm and stuffy.' I started north at a light trot. 'So, like I was saying, if I'm going to do something, I go all in. No half-measures for me.'

'Nothing wrong with that, Mr Helmqvist. It's just that you seem to be good at a lot of things.'

'Well, the PI racket isn't exactly genius level work; you just have to be observant.'

'What about all this tech stuff? I mean the suit and all your computer skills ain't something you just pick up off the street.'

'I have the army to thank for that. When I reported for training, they noticed that I had some aptitude with computer programming and whatnot. After basic training, they assigned me to Encryption and Cyber Espionage. Once there, they taught me all sorts of things

– things that could get a person in a lot of trouble if used inappropriately.'

'So you did ECE the whole two years of your Oblig?' he replied.

Oblig was short for 'obligatory service' – two years of mandatory military service all New Londoners were required to perform the year they graduated high school or on their 18th birthday if they finished early. Most people did it without complaint – even if the entire concept didn't make a whole lot of sense. We don't have any natural enemies on Mars, and any direct hostility should be detected long before it arrives.

However, those facts don't change the reality that we enjoy a rather tenuous living situation. Punch a sufficient number of holes in enough of the domes and we all learn what it literally means to be a fish out of water. An army, I suppose, makes us feel like nothing could ever happen as long as we have a fighting force to prevent it. That might be naïve but it wouldn't be the first time mankind has been levelled with such a charge.

Anyway, it gave us something to do before we went on to university or whatever else people do when they leave school. Some even stay in the army and make a career out of it.

'Four years,' I replied. 'I stayed on for another two because I enjoyed it so much.'

'Damn,' Steve said. 'I worked in the motor pool for my two years then got the hell outta there.'

'Nothing wrong with tha— I have company… Gotta go.' The faint sound of voices echoed down the tunnel. I checked my watch and killed my light.

Eight minutes. Not bad for the public sector at this time of night.

In near total darkness, I barely saw the faint outline of the connecting tunnel of my next turn. I ducked into it and picked up the pace as much as I dared. Behind me, the workers' lamps bounced wildly off the walls, ceiling and floor. The thud of their work boots resonated up and down the corridor as some of them set off in my general direction. Two of them took the same left I had a moment ago. Their lights bobbed up and down while they examined metre after metre of grime-encrusted conduit for signs of obvious damage.

I tiptoed past my exit hatch and continued down the passageway. I couldn't be certain how thorough these guys might be. After a couple hundred metres, though, I crouched behind some pipe work and waited. The edge of darkness halted. The maintenance guys had stopped at the next access point.

Not quite so thorough.

The two workers from the Transit Safety Administration hovered at the edge of my night-vision range. From the chatter I could pick up, they reported everything was all clear at the manhole cover I planned to use. The workers milled about for a few minutes before retracing their steps. I waited until the glow from their lamps and the sound of their boots vanished in the darkness before returning to the hatch.

I shimmied up the ladder to the manhole cover and switched on my visor's small pen lamp. No EMP this time because I wouldn't have eight minutes and the police would definitely get involved on a second alarm.

To free up my hands, I attached myself to the metal rung of the ladder with a lanyard and hook on my belt and had a good look at my next challenge. The set-up was pretty simple. Two remotely controlled automated bolts secured the cover. The male-end of the bolt and the control system was attached to the roof of the tunnel. A pair of female ends that secured the locks in place were welded on to the bottom of the metal disk at the three and nine position. So long as I could override the control system, the locks would open automatically and I could make my escape.

I fished a cable out of a compartment in my belt and clamped the end with a piggyback connector onto one of the remote control wires. The other end I plugged into the left index finger of my glove. I could now access the Transit Authorities' computer system with the touch screen on my MAX smartwatch.

This was not the first time I had infiltrated their network but tonight it took me longer than expected. They must have had a system upgrade recently. Once I was in, though, I still needed to locate the hatch directly above me. It all took time but I managed to figure it out in the end. A short but definitive *clunk* informed me of my success.

I stowed my gear and lifted the lid enough to get a good look around. With nothing in sight, I pushed the heavy lid aside and crawled out into another alley.

Quickly, I slid the cover back into place. Despite my care, the lid clanged down with too much force for my liking. The distinct sound of metal on metal echoed through the alley. I froze in place as the seconds ticked by. The sewer boffins had to have heard the calamity as well.

I inched back into the darkness and waited. But no one came. No sirens. No hard hats popping up from the depths below. Maybe they'd already left the tunnel system. Maybe it was luck: *that thin wire between survival and disaster.*

12

MARA Corp had two main buildings in RD1. A squat, three-storey research and design facility dominated the northern half of the compound. Next to it stood the taller, and more elegant, corporate headquarters. At a total of four floors higher than the R&D building, it came as close to the apex of a dome as any structure in the city.

After I took in the full scope of my 40-metre obstacle, I slunk back into the alley to plan my next moves. It took me several minutes to figure out what I needed to do. Kitterman's office sat on the top floor behind the softly glowing blue 'C' of the company's name. A service door from the executive building, which opened out onto the R&D building's roof, constituted my best point of entry.

The only things standing in my way were an 8-metre-tall brick wall enclosing the joint, getting onto the roof of the R&D building, bypassing the door's biometric and keypad lock, avoiding detection by cameras and security guards alike and cracking the office door of one of the smartest people in the known galaxy.

More than ever I needed Pam. I had the skill set to pull this off. I knew that much. But she was my safety blanket. She always had my back and never made a mistake. However, I also knew I couldn't contact her. To do so would be one more connection to me and this break-in.

Connections. Limiting collateral damage. Culpable deniability. All words used to justify the actions of a man about to commit a felony of the first degree.

A client who came to me in good faith and the belief that I could find the answers to her questions.

A girl who knows I'm up to something tonight and willing to lie about it if necessary.

A cab driver I met just the other day and dragged into my scheme.

And an assistant whose entire life occurred within the limited confines of my office.

A trail of crumbs left for anyone smart enough to follow.

No mistakes and no more crumbs.

According to the schematics, I could piggyback onto MARA Corp's entire network from the security keypad outside the door I intended to use. Cameras, employee files, as well as their fingerprints and guard schedules. Everything. All I needed to do was hop over a wall and up onto a roof in a suit I'd never really used.

What could possibly go wrong?

The simple answer: a lot.

I edged back to the sidewalk and scanned the area. *All clear.* I sucked in some courage and bolted across the street. Three metres before reaching the perimeter wall, I clenched both my fists and engaged the rockets. I shot over it in a nice graceful arc. A short burst to control my descent and I touched down with surprising dexterity.

Four strides later, I fired the jets with too much gusto and hurtled upwards like a nine-pounder shot from the *Queen Anne's Revenge.* I cut the jets and plummeted towards the R&D roof with all the poise of a meteor.

To avoid serious injury, I powered up the levitation system of the boots about a metre before crashing into the roof and it worked – sort of. Without a stabilisation system, the cushion created by the boots caused me to pitch backwards like Chaplin on a banana peel. Spreadeagled and staring up at the dome, I fought through the pain and hoisted myself up into a crouching position. I switched on the thermal imaging in my visor just in time to catch the outline of a person on the other side of the exterior wall, walking towards the roof access door.

In spite of my spine feeling like it had been broken, and the refusal of my lungs to function, I scrambled for the door. Not the best hiding place, but at the very least, the guard might only poke their head out for a quick peek. I had to chance it. If not, this enterprise was over before it even began.

The door opened seconds after I made it to the wall. I held the same breath I had struggled so hard to find moments ago and caught a glimpse of the guard in profile. Could I take this guy? Probably, but not without him seeing me. I could beat him senseless but he'd remember a lunatic in a black super-suit. And he'd talk. To his supervisor. To Kitterman. To the cops. Who knew? But no one outside the military should have a get-up like this one. The account of such a rare encounter would be one more crumb in a growing trail that led right to the tip of my shoes.

Fortunately, the metal barrier clicked shut before my fight *and* flight instinct had a chance to exert full control over me. I exhaled softly as I turned to watch his heat signature drift down the corridor and beyond my field of vision.

The upshot to having the crap scared out of me was that the guard left a handprint on the rail of the door's corrugated metal landing. I scanned his thumbprint onto the thumb of my glove. Once I had it, I compared it against the company's employee database. After a few seconds, I had his name, his ID number, his access codes – everything.

I stole up to the keypad and set to work infiltrating MARA Corp's network. Minutes later, I had all I needed to control the hallway cameras and get inside. The door opened silently on well-oiled hinges and I slipped into the building.

A quick review of the schematics showed me a central staircase I could use to make my ascent to the top floor. I turned the cameras in my area away from my path to the stairwell, adjusted the temperature of my suit to match the thermal sensors, and crept as quietly as two kittens down the corridor to the next of a never-ending series of doors between me and Kitterman's office.

As I entered the stairwell, the door shut louder than I would have liked.

'Anyone there?'

From the distance and the echo, the voice came from two floors below me. Without looking, I sprinted up the stairs, taking two at a time and sticking to the wall as best I could, using the noise made by the guard as he lumbered upwards to cover my own footsteps. The fella below me must have proceeded with some caution because I reached the top before he'd made it to three. I quickly reset the cameras I had moved and prayed no one noticed.

'Phil, this is Walt. Do you copy?'

'Yeah, I copy. What's up?' drifted up to me in faint reply.

'I'm in the central stairwell and I heard a door close. You haven't noticed anything suspicious, have you?'

I could make out the offending item in question opening and closing as he spoke; testing it liked he'd never used one before. I caught the end of a leg and shoe before it disappeared from view. He must have stepped into the hallway to have a look around. I used the opportunity to reposition the camera outside the door next to me and the one near Mara Kitterman's office. The third floor door opened again precisely at the same moment I dashed through the matching one four floors above him.

'Nothing? Roger that, Phil. Maybe I imagined it. I'm heading up to four now. Out,' I heard Walt say into his comm. before I let this door close – much more quietly this time.

I stalked down the seventh floor corridors and reached Mara's door without incident. Another locked door greeted me. Don't get me wrong, I assumed the door would have a lock; it's standard protocol for these corporate types. But this shit was getting old.

Blueprints and schematics will only get a person so far. They don't, for instance, tell you who might have access to the office of one of the most influential people on this little red planet. Guards and cleaning crew made sense so I started there. I already had the fingerprints and chip ID from the guy who had stepped out on R&D's roof earlier. They worked once, so why not again? I placed my thumb on the scanner with his print still loaded into it.

Success!

The sound of the lock mechanism might as well have been a

chorus of angels' singing. At long last, I had reached my prize. Kitterman's *sanctum sanctorum* was nothing more than a doorknob turn away.

13

Once inside her office, I relocked the door and scanned the room for additional security measures. The schematics didn't show any but I hadn't come all this way to trip at the finish line.

Despite the fact that reality matched the construction drawings, a sense of relief did not wash over me. Instead, I stuck to the walls, away from the centre of the room, eyeing it like the heart of some sort of abandoned Inca temple waiting to drop a giant boulder on the careless. Keeping to the perimeter also gave me a chance to take in the office with more detail.

A conference table with six chairs dominated one part of the large room. Mara's imposing Georgian-style desk and a high-backed executive model occupied the other half. Beyond these two features, the room contained little in terms of decor. The wall opposite the door was one large pane of smart-glass overlooking RD1. Expensive-looking wood panelled the lower half of the other three walls. Painted some version of white, the upper halves of the walls reflected the light cast by the corporate logo, giving the place a soft, warm glow.

Three pieces of art adorned the interior walls. A portrait of her father and another of her mother hung near the conference table. They looked like silent mediators who presided solemnly over every meeting Mara had in this office. The other painting took me by surprise: an original Bengt Oscar.

His work reflected a distrust of a world becoming increasingly reliant on technology. Bengt Oscar used bold colour combinations and strong brush techniques to create haunting and complex allegories of a world subsumed by the one thing it loved so dearly: high-tech gadgetry.

Like countless other artists before him, Bengt Oscar enjoyed very little success during his lifetime. Most people deemed his work harsh and inaccessible. However, within the last couple of decades, his pieces started to gain popularity and now sell for impressive sums at auction.

I moved around Kitterman's desk to get a closer look at the painting. I switched on my visor's penlight in order to see better. It was stupid of me to do so, but I doubted I'd ever have another opportunity to see one of his paintings outside of a museum.

The piece contained a fairly simple landscape that featured a group of leafless birch trees standing along a dirt road in the foreground. All around the trees and along the road, high grass filled the canvas in a jumbled mass of browns, auburns, reds and goldenrod. The high grass gave way to pale yellow strokes that resembled a field of wheat. In the far background, a line of trees separated the golden field from the dulled orange sky with indistinct shades of green.

Without a hint of distorted machinery, or anything pointing to his disdain for a self-destructive modernity, it must have been one of his earlier works. My reverie and appreciation of the painting was brought to a sudden, panic-inducing conclusion by the sound of Kitterman's office door unlocking.

Another freakin' guard? How many times? How many times was this going to happen before I could get my ass outta here?

I killed the penlight and crawled under the desk. Fortunately, the front panel of the Georgian desk went all the way down to the floor. I'd be safe from detection so long as the newcomer didn't come all the way around for a thorough peek.

Trails of light bounced around the wall behind me and streaked across the Bengt Oscar. Like peals of lightning, each flash gave the birch trees in the painting a brief but menacing appearance. The gentle creak of well-worn shoes matched the soft thud of rubber soles as the light and the guard walked to the centre of the room. By the heaviness of the footsteps, I could tell it was a guy.

My God, how these guards had hounded me the entire night without their knowing. An unintentional pursuit from rooftop to top floor. A game of hide and seek that only I knew we were playing. It might have been funny if I wasn't so damn tired.

I told myself I didn't get into this business so I could wear super-suits and leap from building to building like a crime-fighting avenger. I wore a shirt and tie to work. I followed leads, my gut, the evidence and got the job done. This b-and-e and hacking your way into a high-profile place was for someone else.

But not for me.

Says the guy with the super-suit, who has already committed several felonies. I bought the lie though. Desperate people will buy anything if they think it'll get them out of a jam.

I poured all of my energy into pleading with cosmic forces to stop the guard before he made it to the side of the desk with a clear view of me balled up underneath it. And it worked. At mid-room he came to a standstill, bounced his light around the place a few more times, turned and left. The lock reset and I sat there, waiting and listening. After a few minutes of all quiet, I pushed Kitterman's chair out and peeked my head over the desk. I had the office to myself once again.

Another quick check of the schematics confirmed that a safe should be in the wall behind the painting. I eased the picture down off the wall, and found a thick metal door with a touch screen.

'Last hurdle,' I told myself quietly before removing the touch screen's four set-screws, which gave me access to a motherboard and a connection port.

The complexity of the code for the safe lock almost beat me. I nearly called it quits. The design was intentionally convoluted. Probably to slow down a box man like me and give the guards time to respond. Those last words sunk in and I redoubled my efforts. Through the fatigue of a long-ass day and fear of Walt, or Phil, or someone else barging in at any moment, my brain and fingers raced through codes, combinations and every trick in the book.

A telltale click alerted me to my success. Despite the small door being about 5 centimetres thick, it opened outwards on its internal hinges easily. I flicked on my visor penlight again and had a closer inspection of the safe's contents.

A stack of important-looking papers and folders partially hid my prize: a datapad measuring 10 centimetres by 10 centimetres. Without knowing what sort of security protocols the device contained, I knew I had to take it with me. I had to risk Kitterman discovering its absence over the risk of another guard coming into her office while I tried to access it through the FE9's computer.

I slid it out of the safe and into my backpack. With the safe closed, and the painting back in its spot, I gave the place a once over to ensure nothing looked out of place.

The thought of retracing my steps filled me with dread. Instead, I opted to go up to the roof and try my luck with the jetpack again. At Kitterman's office door, I repositioned the hallway cameras to give me a clear shot back to the stairwell.

By the grace of all that is good and holy, I made it to the roof exit without running into any more guards. One more alarm disabled and I basked in the calm Martian night, feeling like a man just released from prison. Now to get the hell out of here and back to my much-missed bed.

I snuck up to the edge of the roof and took a peek at R&D below me. All clear. With no idea who might be where, I vaulted over the edge and dropped like a stone. The jets kicked in a few metres above R&D's roof as I balled my hands into tight fists. I landed with some confidence-inducing grace and jogged to the edge closest to the alley I had made the first jump from earlier.

A voice came over my earpiece and nearly gave me a heart attack.

'Mr Helmqvist?' It was my wheelman.

'Yeah, Steve,' I said in a low voice. 'Everything alright?'

'I dunno. You tell me. It's getting kinda late.'

I checked my watch. 4:30am. 'Jesus! That late already? I'm nearly out of here. I'll call in a few minutes for a pick up.'

'You got it,' he replied on the back end of a yawn.

Twenty metres from the edge of the building, I tried to visualise the next jump in my head like an Olympic athlete. I went through each step until I felt comfortable enough to trust my instincts. I took off at a measured pace and picked up speed as I neared the end of the real estate. Rockets engaged, I soared through the air like a tiny, black missile.

I cleared the perimeter wall and flew straight at the space between the two buildings. My altitude ensured I'd not be seen by cameras. However, my speed carried me too far. I shot into the alley like an errant Roman candle. I attempted various acrobatic manoeuvres to right myself, fired the boosters, activated the shoes and did everything I could do to not kill myself.

In that regard, I did succeed.

I didn't die but I got banged up pretty badly. When I turned on the boots' electromagnetic levitation system in a failed attempt at a controlled descent, I sort of bounced along the pavement like a kid on a pogo stick and ricocheted into the building on my left. I hit it awkwardly with my elbow, which sent me into a spin. I landed on my right knee and fell over on my right side with no amount of grace.

Surprisingly, I could flex my elbow without problem. My knee, on the other hand, hurt like hell. I could bend it, so no structural damage. But it felt like someone was stabbing it with a screwdriver. I rolled over to a sitting position and attempted to stand. I got there in the end but no way could I make a mad dash through the alleyways to meet Steve where he had dropped me off.

'Steve,' I groaned into the comm. unit.

'You alright, Mr Helmqvist? You sound like you're in pain.'

'I've been better. But let's just say that I'm no rocket man, that's for sure.'

'Who?'

'Never mind. Can you pick me up on Corporation East? I'm about midway down the block. I'll flash you with a penlight as you approach.'

'You got it. Be there in a coupla minutes.'

I hobbled up to the entrance of the alley and waited in the shadows. True to his word, about two minutes later I saw the headlights of an LTI city cab. I flashed it with the light on my visor.

'Stop in the alley, if you can. I don't want to be seen.'

The taxi turned into the narrow space between the buildings. The rear door opened enough for me to wiggle into the back seat.

'What happened?' he asked as he backed out onto the street.

'I tried to get too cute and it bit me in the ass.' I pulled the helmet off and threw it on the seat next to me.

'What?'

'I landed on my knee funny but it's not too worse for wear.'

'Ice always helps. Where to? Back to Commercial?'

'Yeah, but before we go, I need you to do me one more favour.'

'What's that?'

'Can you get my clothes? I left them in another alley over off of Franklin.'

'No problem.' Steve made an immediate left and headed towards Franklin.

Less than 10 minutes later, we were on our way back to the CD. I dressed as best as my bum leg would allow. I stowed the helmet and the gloves back in their storage space in the backpack. The storage device, I shoved in my jacket pocket.

We drove in silence. I caught the reflection of my smile in the cab's window. Safely away from the immediacy of the danger of being caught, my adrenaline surged. Injured knee aside, I had to admit it was quite a rush hopping around in a suit made for heroes. All that complaining in Kitterman's office was the fear talking. Truth be told, I dug it. Visions of cleaning up the streets of New London drifted through my mind. My city had a relatively low crime rate, but what about a zero crime rate? There was a thought…

We had just exited the avenue that connected RD1 with CD when Steve broke the silence.

'Did you want to stop by your office?'

And just like that, the adrenaline washed out of my body and fatigue smothered me. I could save the city another day.

'Nah, just take me home. I think that we've been out long enough tonight. Don't you agree?'

'Completely.'

'Drop me off around the corner from my place, about mid-block, and I'll walk the rest of the way there.'

'You sure about that with your knee and all?'

'Not in the least,' I responded with a wry grin. 'But I still need to maintain the illusion of being home all night and that means avoiding any cameras.'

'You're the boss.'

The LTI stopped near the alley behind my building. I paid the fee from the dummy account and tacked on a large tip.

'That's way too much, Mr Helmqvist,' he said when he looked at the reader in his part of the cabin.

'You earned it. Thanks for not abandoning me tonight.' And remember my generosity if the heat comes down on us.

'Well, if you insist,' he said, as he turned in his seat to face me better. 'And give me a call any time you need a driver.'

'I definitely will.'

I extracted myself from the LTI with some care. The pain in my knee had settled into a dull throb that made it bearable.

The cab pulled away and took a left at the next intersection. I limped along in the same direction but took a right instead.

At the alley next to my building, I ducked in and looked up at the fire escape ladder with some amount of consternation; leaping up to grab the bottom rung most assuredly meant more pain.

I was right. I managed the jump badly and the landing sent a jolt of pain up my leg like someone had jabbed a handful of needles into my knee. I wanted to howl at the top of my lungs. Instead, I bore it with tears in my eyes and a silent grunt.

I managed to hobble up the ladder and reach the landing outside my bathroom. One more easy system hack and I was, at long last, home sweet home. Once inside, I sat on the bathtub edge, stripped down to my birthday suit and gave my knee a closer inspection.

It was swollen and discoloured, but not too bad. The FE9's kneepad had absorbed most of the impact. Nothing a regimen of painkillers couldn't sort out in a few days, or weeks.

I fumbled about in the medicine cabinet until I found a prescription from a martial arts training injury. The label said not to take more than two at a time. I gulped three down with mouthfuls of water straight from the tap. I had a look at myself in the mirror and I wished I hadn't. Nothing a shower couldn't remedy tomorrow.

In the living room, I jammed the spy gear and the datapad into a gym bag and hobbled towards the bedroom. Erica was sleeping quietly with her back to the doorway.

In the soft glow of the early morning light, she looked even more beautiful. I dumped my clothes in a hamper, grabbed a pair of boxers off the floor, changed into them and slid in next to Erica.

She stirred but quickly settled back into a deep sleeping pattern. I lay on my back and stared at the ceiling; smiling once again. For better or worse, I had made it through the night. I had broken into one of the most sophisticated tech facilities on Mars and made it out alive.

14

A late night filled with a lot of close calls, and a whole lot of pain, should have trumped anything attempting to pull me from my mini-coma. However, the sensation of gentle bites on my neck and ear-lobes, the feeling of Erica's soft curves and a silky smooth leg draped over mine, eased me into the conscious world.

'Morning.' Her warm breath sent delightful chills down my spine. 'You're here.'

She grinned and cocked an ear. 'No sirens. No one banging on the door. I guess your night went well?'

'Well enough, but not without incident.'

'Oh?'

'I banged my knee up.'

'You poor thing.' Erica pushed me playfully flat onto my back. 'I'm no doctor, but I heard bed rest and a distraction are excellent cures for this type of injury.'

She slid her hand across my chest and down under the sheets. I tensed up.

'You heard this, did you?'

'I did.'

Before I could say anything else, Erica slid on top of me and took complete command of the situation. I moved my hands up the side of her thighs and hips but she did the rest. And she was right – I forgot all about the pain in my knee.

When we finished, Erica rolled off me, breathing heavily. A thin layer of sweat glistened on her body. I rolled over on my right side. My knee took that opportunity to remind me that I played pinball with it last night. I swallowed the pain and ran the fingers of my left hand over her stomach.

'I'm not sure my knee is fixed, but maybe with a few more treatments like that, I might be one hundred per cent in a few weeks' time.'

Her laugh sounded like a song. 'We should do something about that then, but for the moment, I am absolutely starving!'

'I know a great place for breakfast.'

'And it isn't where I work?'

'Surprise, surprise, it isn't.'

'Then let's go! Dinner felt like a lifetime ago.'

We threw on the same outfits we had on the night before and headed out the door.

After a delicious brunch, we parted ways at her doorstep with a kiss and a promise to do it again once I had wrapped up my current case.

Stereophonics' *A New Stereophonic Sound Spectacular* played in the background as I negotiated my way through traffic back to the Commercial District. Events from the night before superimposed themselves over the very same streets, buildings and monuments as I cruised by them. How different everything looked in the noonday sun.

My FE9 barely fit into the hidden compartment in the Griffon's trunk. It wasn't my top choice of hiding spots, but I couldn't risk leaving it in my apartment or my office. The break-in at MARA Corp might end up knocking on either, or both, doors with a search warrant. I had to gamble on them overlooking my car as a possible place to investigate under reasonable circumstances.

'Why hello, Pam,' I grunted as I pushed my way through the front door. Every step to my office was accompanied by the sensation of a nail gun to my knee.

'Good afternoon,' she replied after slight delay. 'Based on your gait, it appears you have suffered damage to the synovial joint of your right leg.'

'How nice of you to notice.' I hobbled to her desk and took my usual spot on the right corner. 'Any phone calls?'

'No, sir.'

'Any visitors, like the police? Or the army? Or better yet, a robot army?'

She responded with her unusual brand of contemptuous silence.

'My mission last night was a success.'

'You obtained the datapad?'

I produced it from my jacket pocket. 'Hey! I told you to scrub the events of last night from your memory banks.'

'I took it as a suggestion and decided not to comply.'

'A suggestion? Christ! If the police confiscate you, they'll know I did it!' Professional privilege did not extend to androids any more than it did to a toaster.

She shrugged. I swear to God she actually shrugged. 'What's done is done. It will be in your best interest not to alert the police, or anyone else, to your illicit activities.'

Anger would have been an acceptable response. Instead, I bust my gut laughing. *What's done is done.* The absurdity of an android employing such a well-heeled idiom was too much.

'I'll do my best.' With my index finger and thumb, I swiped tears from my eyes. 'Speaking of, I will need your help running interference while I access this device. My guess: this thing has a sniffer that'll send a traceable signal to Kitterman as soon as it's powered-up.'

'Very well, sir. I will begin running countermeasures when you are ready.'

She looked back at her monitor, fingers hovering over the keyboard ready to get started. I limped back to my office and eased myself into my chair.

'Begin running interference and bouncing our ISP,' I called through the intercom; no shouting today.

'I have already started. You may proceed when you are ready.'

'What would I do without you?'

'Should I answer that, or is it rhetorical?'

'Rhetorical.'

In case the datapad had some sort of RFI locator built into it, I placed the device in a Faraday Cage of my own design, connecting it to a WildCat port on the inside of the box. The cage, I plugged into my computer. When I did, it hummed to life. At the same time, the datapad lit up with soft glowing lines of blue LED that raced around its edges. A few seconds later, 'MARA Corporation' appeared on my screen in the same block lettering I had seen on the building last night.

'Detect anything?'

'Yes, sir. The device attempted to send out a locating signal the moment you powered it up. However, I muted the signal before it left the office.'

'Good girl.'

'You have used this phrase before and I do not understand why. I am not a girl, sir. I am modelled after a human female.'

'Thanks, Pam. I hadn't noticed. Now be quiet. I need to concentrate.'

The determined banging of keys echoed through the intercom.

'The device is protected by an asymmetrical algorithm,' I called out. 'This might take a while.'

'Is there anything that I can do to help?'

'Nothing more than you already are doing.'

It took me about an hour to crack the public key in the encryption. That left the private one (or as people like to refer to it – the *secret* key – to give it an air of mystery). Still, I counted this as a minor victory.

'Mr Helmqvist?'

'Yes, Pam,' I said as I typed away furiously.

'I thought that you should know that the device attempted to flag itself across multiple platforms. They have been successfully suppressed.'

'That would be because I unlocked one of the keys. Expect it again when I get the second.'

'Yes, sir.'

Anticipation coursed through every fibre of my being. I was moments away from learning the truth about Mara Kitterman.

Much to my surprise, it only took 45 minutes to get past the second password and unlock the files.

'I'm in!'

'Congratulations,' Pam said over the intercom with what I think was an attempt at enthusiasm.

'Thanks. I couldn't have done it without you. Were there any more attempts to locate the device?'

'There were but I routed them to a server on Ganymede and then bounced the signal to every major Earth city.'

'Well done! I'm going to access the files now. Standby.'

I pulled up the file system on my machine and found a main directory plus an executable file. Nested within the main file resided a whole horde of subdirectories filled with terabytes of information. The sheer volume was staggering, and not one obvious clue to direct me down the correct path.

A cursory search yielded nothing. A file labelled 'UN Bombing' would have been very handy. I didn't even find anything of interest around the time of the attack in Manhattan. That left the executable file as my last hope.

I double-clicked on it and the word *Transilience* appeared on the monitor, followed by a 3D model of a featureless man who looked like department store window dressing. After a few revolutions on an invisible axis, it shifted to the left side of the screen. On the right, data cascaded down the screen.

As best I could tell, it was technical information related to the figure next to it. By all appearances, I hadn't stolen a smoking gun from under Kitterman's nose. Instead, I had taken her latest project like some piece of shit industrial spy. Like a common thief.

All my hard work and the risk getting into her office and I grab the wrong storage device. I broke the law on so many levels; not to mention the abuse of my poor knee. I picked Executive when I probably should've picked R&D. I bet the house on red and it came up black. Karma and Irony both gave me the one finger salute.

To make matters worse, the damn thing sat there, mocking me with its pulsing blue glow. It took the will of a titan not to smash the thing to tiny pieces. My God how I wanted to and probably should have.

But I didn't.

It wasn't mine and I felt more than a little shame because I had taken someone's intellectual property; even if I suspected them of mass murder.

Once my rage subsided, I simply unplugged the datapad.

'Alright, Pam, we should be out of danger,' I said out loud while I continued to watch the machine. 'Do one last sweep to make sure we're clear.'

'No evidence of polling. I believe that we are safe,' she replied after a few seconds.

I slumped back in my chair. Disappointment, mental exhaustion and hunger hit me from all sides. I needed to get out of the office. So I scooped up the device, my suit jacket and hat and went into the conference room where I kept disposable lab gloves, various wipes and sprays. I gave the device a thorough cleaning and ran it under a UV light. Once I was convinced it didn't have any of my prints or DNA on it, I slid the datapad into a plastic bag and sealed it tight.

Even though I had resolved not to destroy the storage unit, I didn't have a clear plan as to how to get rid of it. My best bet would be to get it into the hands of the police. How to achieve that anonymously, however, posed some serious problems. Forensic scientists could find so much these days. They made it nearly impossible to get away with anything.

I walked out into Pam's area of the office, holding the bag in my glove-covered hands like it might explode any second.

'What will you do with the device?' Her gaze shifted from me to the bag.

'I thought that maybe you could drop it off, anonymously, on the steps of Metro HQ sometime later tonight.'

Her eyes widened at the thought. '*Me?!*'

'Yes, you. You're perfect. You have no fingerprints to leave a traceable path back to this office and I doubt that anyone would recognise you on the street. You never leave here.'

'That's just it, I never leave here.' She moved her gaze from me to around the office. 'This is where I belong. Besides, they would know. The police and, in all probability, MARA Corporation can track all androids from a central location. It is part of the protocol required by New London law. My ID signature might trigger some sort of notification to alert the police of my presence as soon as I neared the station. Far too risky for me to leave here.'

'Damn! Of course. How could I forget that?'

'I'm not sure, Mr Helmqvist, but it is the law.'

'Again, rhetorical.'

'Oh.'

'Take an envelope big enough for this package and print "Deliver to MARA Corporation. Do not open" on it.'

When she finished, I jammed the package and another pair of lab gloves in a satchel.

'Okay, Pam,' I said. 'I'll ditch this some place as far away from here as New London permits. You're off the hook.'

Again, I would swear that she relaxed her entire composure in a gesture of relief.

'Thanks again for the help today. I couldn't have done this without you.'

'You're welcome, Mr Helmqvist. Are you done for the day?'

'I think so. I need a break and some food. I thought I'd catch a film at the Art House. They're showing Hitchcock's last picture in a one-night engagement. Maybe I'll find some inspiration there.'

I checked my smartwatch. The film started at 8pm and the Art House was only a few blocks from my office. That gave me plenty of time to get up to some mischief and be back before the intro credits began to roll.

I set off with a vague idea of where I should ditch Kitterman's storage device. Either the IM or Res 3. Both places the cops would expect to find it. I meandered through the industrial sector but nothing jumped out at me. Eventually, I found an alley I knew from growing up in Res 3 on an avenue with missing street cameras. I hopped out of the Griffon, checked for an all clear, and threw the package down the alley. It glided through the air like a Frisbee and skipped off the ground with a dull thud. I retreated back to my car and said goodbye to the old neighbourhood without a glance in the rearview mirror.

I lived close to the Art House Theatre and decided to hobble there. It was a pleasant night for a leisurely walk, but then again, it's always pleasant when you live under a dome. I arrived at the cinema with enough time to spare to enjoy a whisky neat from the lobby bar.

The movie was good, not quite your usual Hitchcock, and hit pretty close to home. The actor-turned-private-investigator boyfriend felt strangely autobiographical. I could've been Lumley; some poor schmuck drawn into a vocation entirely unsuited to him. I could also see a little bit of Charlotte Rennick in the phony psychic. A comedy hidden behind a thinly veiled mystery sounded about right. Anyway, when I walked out of the theatre and headed towards the nearest Underground station, I felt a little less dour.

I strolled into the 3rd Street Lounge and stopped in my tracks. Instead of the usual sad sacks leaning on the bar, a crowd of twenty-some-things filled the joint. And the music didn't sound like something played from speakers. My gaze shifted left. Five actual human beings played their way through Woody Shaw's 'Traffic Jam'. About a dozen lookers and gees swung to the music, doing their damnedest to rub the polish off the parquet.

A quintet in the 3rd Street.

A sure sign of the end of times. And, lo, there was a great earth-quake; and the sun became black as sackcloth of hair, and the moon became as blood.

A group of hipsters sat in my usual spot so I eased up to the bar. Curt slid a highball in front of me. The tonic fizzled away merrily.

'What gives, Curt? I take one night off and I come back to find you've added some class to this dive.'

'I know, right?' He looked around like he had no idea how it had happened. 'What do you think?'

'Aside from my spot being taken, it's good.' The band had moved on to an upbeat version of 'Perfidia' in a style best called Brubeck. 'And for a bunch of kids, the five on the stage can play. How in the hell did you find them?'

'They're music students from the university. I pop down there every now and then hoping to find someone willing to play here. These five agreed and I guess they told their friends about it.'

Curt seemed to downplay this but I knew it was a big deal for him.

He and I went back to our university days. We were in the same year at the University of New London's Law School. He and I graduated with honours and passed the bar exam on our first attempt. However, he never practised law. I, on the other hand, spent longer than I care to admit as a prosecutor for the city of New London. Curt chased a dream and opened this bar. He's even managed to get live music in here. I followed expectations and became disillusioned and bitter. Thank God Curt did what he did. 3rd Street has been my home away from home since the moment he opened the doors.

'Well, keep the drinks coming. It's been a long day.'

Somewhere in the second set, the gin started to take me down memory lane. The storage device. Transilience. The failure to find anything worthwhile. Setbacks. The character, Fran, from the movie. Charlotte Rennick.

In the background, the trumpeter poured his soul into 'Freddie Freeloader'. I tried to enjoy it but couldn't shake the image of Rennick sitting next to me in this same place a few days ago. Another gin and tonic later, I had the touch screen on my smartwatch out and activating the tracking programme on the earrings I gave her. The blinking light placed her in MARA Corp's R&D building. Not unusual for a person to work late, but it struck me as odd for some reason.

By the third set, I was on doubles and checking my watch every 30 seconds. Nothing changed. Rennick's dot continued to flash in the R&D building. During the band's final break, Curt ushered me into a cab and sent me on my way. Through years of practice, I made it up to my apartment, crawled out of my clothes and into bed.

On the nightstand next to me, the red spot that represented my client pulsed like a heartbeat in the exact same place it had the entire night. I struggled to focus on the light for as long as possible; hoping to see it move some place… any place. But it didn't. Somewhere in the R&D building Rennick stayed. Blinking. Blinking. Blinking.

15

The indistinct outlines of fellow commuters faded in and out as I rushed past them. I took the stairs down to the Red Line in pairs. The world sped up and slowed down on a whim. Sometimes moving at sub-lightspeed and, at other times, like someone had hit the pause button on a remote. I dashed through the entrance barrier and raced to the correct platform.

I got there well ahead of the train's announced arrival time. And yet I could see it parked on the Blue Line. I ran like the wind for the nearest set of stairs. But before I could make it, the train disappeared, vanishing into thin air. A voice over the PA system called out its departure from the Green Line.

Down another set of stairs, around a corner, down more steps. Relief washed over me when I saw that it hadn't left yet. I sprinted for the nearest car and slipped in before the door closed on the heels of its all too familiar polyphonic tone.

When I looked around for a place to sit, I discovered I was alone. I peered through the rear window into the next car – empty. As far as I could tell in both directions, they were all empty.

No one else on this train but me.

I took a seat in the middle and stared out the window. Countryside, with lush, green forests and wide hills, rolled into view as we left the city. The world scrolling past me belonged to Emerson or Coleridge, not the dusty, harsh sameness of the Martian landscape. Everything seemed crisp and new, like an early spring day on one of those Earth nature programmes. After what felt like hours, however, the scenery outside became hazy as if some indefinable pall had settled over the landscape.

Eventually, the train stopped.

And, I mean stopped stopped.

End of the line.

Time to get off.

The doors opened.

The power and lights went out.

Curiosity compelled me to exit.

I stepped out onto a wooden platform into a world devoid of colour. A lake in the far-off distance and more hills beyond it blended together in dull sepia tones.

Without any warning, the entire perspective of my dream changed. My face, a mask of confusion, filled up the entire scene like some sort of movie close-up. Suddenly, I began to shrink in the view as the camera tracked away from me. Another spin of my perspective, and through my own eyes I saw the lake rushing closer to me as I sailed through the sky as effortlessly as a hawk. The ground below me passed by impossibly fast. The surface of the lake grew larger. Fear coursed through every fibre of my being, urging me on to an unknown doom.

An old man, ancient and pale, sat in a boat in the middle of the lake. He wore threadbare clothes, a shabby Tilley fishing hat and a dirty beard. I closed in on the stranger in sweeping 360 revolutions. Each completed turn brought me closer to him until I stopped and stared directly into his sunken eyes.

'Something weird is gonna happen,' he said, not to me but at me, with a sad, quiet voice.

Cut to an image of the lake.

I see myself, naked and lifeless, slowly descending into impossibly black, cold as death water.

Sinking into the murky abyss.

I woke with a start. The icy numbness from the dream chilled me to the core. My head pounded. My stomach lurched. I made a break for the bathroom and dropped to my knees without a second to spare. The pain from doing so never registered.

Each violent spasm of my stomach brought up all of yesterday and anything still in there from the day before. I puked. And I heaved.

I heaved until there was nothing left but bile and the echo of my acid-burned throat in the toilet. My temples throbbed under the strain of keeping all of the grey matter inside.

Eventually, my tank was empty. I clung to the bowl with all the desperation of a man lost at sea. Slow, deep breaths brought with them a sense of calm and allowed me to gather enough strength to crawl into the shower. I managed to turn the water on before slumping against the cool tile wall. Water from the overhead diffuser rained down on me. Heat and steam chased away the chill in my bones, but no amount of water in the world could dispel the image of my body being pulled under in that evil lake.

I limped into the office and found Pam at her desk reading the Mars News Network site. I peered over her shoulder and glanced at the headline: *Police Nab Suspect in Technology Theft.*

My eyes hurt too much to read the article, though. 'Looks like someone didn't follow the instructions on the envelope.'

'Indeed, sir. According to the article, a special task force arrested a man in Residential District 3 early this morning in connection to a break-in "at a high-tech facility".'

'Are there any low-tech facilities these days?'

Pam glossed over the question and went back to reading. I took the bagel and coffee I had picked up on the way to my office and settled in for an afternoon of doing very little.

While I demolished my mid-day breakfast, I used the time to check on Rennick's position. Her dot hadn't moved, or she had left work and returned while I was passed out. Helluva work ethic either way. I didn't risk trying to contact her. I had to trust she would reach out to me.

My assistant's voice over the intercom woke me from an impromptu nap.

'Mr Helmqvist, you have a client.'

'A what?' I replied like the village idiot.

'A client, sir.'

'Oh… right… of course. Give me a second before sending them in.'

I wiped the sleep out of my eyes and met them at the door. I preferred this little ritual to sitting and waiting for them like the school principal expecting the class bully.

The woman who entered was somewhere in her fifties but was trying to pass as a thirty-something. She wore stylish, expensive-looking clothes and even pricier jewellery. You could tell by the look of her that she wanted everyone to know she had money. And with her pert little smile and general air of haughtiness, I also knew that she was probably used to getting her way. I offered her a chair then took my place behind my desk.

She said she needed to have someone investigated. I told her she had come to the right place. I asked who and she said her maid.

'The maid?' I asked without trying to sound too incredulous.

'That's right.'

'Let me guess, she's stealing from you.' I did a quick take from head to neck. The earrings didn't match the necklace. 'Jewellery, am I right?'

Her eyes lit up.

'Why yes! How did you know?'

'I'm a regular Sherlock Holmes.'

I don't think that she appreciated the sarcasm. I pushed for details and she gave them to me. Some of her 'everyday' pieces had started to come up missing for about the past three months. I liked that – everyday pieces. As if we all have 5-carat tennis bracelets to wear when we trudge off to our boring, insignificant lives.

I asked why the maid. It seemed a bit too clichéd to be true. No other possible candidate was her reply.

With my elbows on my desk, I regarded her over interlocked hands and played the scenario out in my mind. She seemed like the type of broad who didn't mind the silent treatment.

'I'm not going to take the case, Mrs Beaumont.'

That was her name, Elizabeth Beaumont, and she belonged to

New London's upper crust. I had seen their name in the papers a few times. The husband, Kendrick, had made a ton of cash in asteroid mining futures. The Beaumonts also had two kids. A son, aged 17, lived at home. He attended private school in Res 1. A daughter. Aged 20. Attended UNL. Lived on campus in what I imagined to be a pretty swanky set-up. I had seen their names in the papers, too. They were the quintessential spoiled brats, who did spoiled brat things with other spoiled brats.

'What do you mean that you won't take the case?' she asked with a hint of indignation. 'I'm sure that I can more than cover your fee.'

'One, if it's stolen goods, it's a police matter. You should call them. Their rates are much more reasonable. And two, I don't think you'll like what an investigation'll turn up.'

'I am quite certain I don't know what you mean, Mr Helmqvist, and I am absolutely certain that I don't like your tone. As for the police, I would rather this matter be handled with discretion. It was wrong for Harriet to take my things but I couldn't possibly stand to see her go to prison over this.'

Man, this was rich. She actually did look offended now. I started to feel like a bit character in a 19th-century morality play.

'My apologies if you don't approve of my tone, I get that a lot. Just the same, I'm not going to take the case. Despite what you may think, or claim, we both know that it isn't Harriet stealing your trinkets, which is probably the real reason you don't want to get the police involved. It might create an awkward situation for you when it gets out to all your well-to-do friends that it wasn't the hired help.'

My money was on the son. He had probably gotten into something beyond what his hefty allowance could afford.

'If you are implying that the thief is a member of my own family, I won't stand for it,' and then she actually stood. I fought back a grin at the irony.

'Fine. Put a surveillance camera in your dressing room and you'll get your answer soon enough. I'd bet the house it's one of your kids.'

That pushed her over the edge.

'You, Mr Helmqvist, are a brute. If this is how you treat all of your customers, then I cannot possibly imagine how you stay in business.'

I had had my fun with her and decided to give her back some of what she had been dishing out. I stood up and affected my own mask of indignation. Maybe I didn't give a rat's ass if she liked me or not, but I had a reputation to protect.

'I do fine, lady. I don't take cases that involve someone trying to pin a pack of lies and false accusations on someone probably too poor to defend themselves properly. Anyway, you don't need a private investigator. You need a family shrink. Fire the maid if you want, see if that stops the thefts. But again, I think we both know how that'll play out. And at the end of the day, all you'll have done is ruined the life of one person, whose only crime is the misfortune of working for your sorry ass.'

Her cheeks flushed with rage and I think that she would have slapped me right then and there if her dignity would have allowed for it. Instead, she turned and marched out of the office without saying so much as a goodbye.

'If every day was like this, I'd probably be in the office more often,' I announced to Pam when she swivelled in her chair to meet my gaze through the communicating doorway. She shook her head in disappointment, and returned to abusing her keyboard.

I sat back at my desk and checked the tracking device. Rennick hadn't left MARA Corp. I decided it best that I did some work and by that I mean I played Sudoku on the computer. Somewhere on my second hard puzzle, I checked the tracker again. Finally, the blinking dot moved, by the looks of it heading towards the IM. The image of the 3rd Street came to mind and where this all began.

Perhaps she wanted to meet me there again.

Never hurts to be optimistic.

16

The expected phone call from Rennick never came. An hour passed and she never called. The display on my smartwatch never lit up with her name and number. And Pam never patched her through on the office line. The tracking device took her all the way to the IM and stopped.

Something didn't feel right. I cross-referenced the location of the dot with a city directory to a factory long since abandoned.

What the hell could she possibly be doing there?

I jotted the address down, grabbed my hat and gave my assistant a heads-up as to what was going on.

I drove like an asshole from the CD to the IM. The simulated exhaust of my Nash Griffon rumbled as I negotiated the car through the very precise matrix of streets and cross-streets. Occasionally I checked my location against the address I had copied down.

As I cruised past an endless collection of abandoned buildings, the scene reminded me of photos I'd seen as a kid of Detroit in a coffee-table book my parents always had out on a side table next to the sofa. Once a pinnacle of human achievement, New London's Industrial and Manufacturing dome was a reminder that our galaxy had become very small, and that there was a virtually unlimited choice of cheap places to set up a business.

The faded sign for 1643 Edison clung to a perimeter fence by a screw too stubborn to let go.

'This must be the place,' I said aloud for the sole purpose of breaking the eerie silence.

The front gate was open – 'missing' would be a more precise term. I guided the Griffon through and cut the engine about 30 metres from the main building. After coasting to a gentle stop, I hopped out and had a better look at the remains of the now-defunct Verne Bottling Company.

High above, a bright flash streaked across the periphery of my vision. I stared up at a perfectly clear afternoon Martian sky. It must have been a malfunction in the biosphere dome. Atmospheric lightning is reserved for places with an actual atmosphere, not here. It didn't rain on Mars and fluffy clouds did not drift idly by inside, or outside, our domed existence. The best we got was violent storms at ground level that spit dust and static electricity as they roamed the countryside like whirling demons.

However, we did have neglect and I suspected they serviced this district only as much as needed in order to prevent a catastrophe. You would never see anything like electrical shorts (or surges) in the domes of the RD1 or Res 1. But then money has the ability to create those types of grand illusions we associate with perfection.

A noise in the factory brought me back to the matter at hand. This didn't look like the kind of joint you'd come to for a meeting. It looked more like a place to dispose of a body, or create a body, or both. I knew Rennick was inside somewhere, but charging in unprepared would make every other mistake I'd made in my life seem like a blessing from God above.

I walked to the back of the car and popped the trunk. With the push of a button, the same secret compartment I'd used to hide my super-suit opened and I surveyed its additional contents – another pair of bracelets, concussion rifle and a second NEEDLE.

The concussion rifle, I tried to hide as best I could behind my leg. I tucked the handcuffs into my belt. I chambered a neurological round in the pistol and slid it into a shoulder holster. For good measure, I stuffed an EMP round in my pocket. I approached the corner of the building and crept along the exterior wall to a rusty old door about 20 metres away.

The sound of glass breaking into hundreds of shards shattered the quiet. The blur of a figure soared out of the window like a stuntman in a summer blockbuster. He hit the ground running. Out of sheer panic, I brought the rifle around and fired from the hip. The gun kicked in my hands but a blast of pure concussive force hit the guy in the right shoulder.

The blast sent him tumbling into a heap of old metal, industrial cable and broken crates. He stood up and took stock of his situation. By the blood running down his arm, I knew he must have nicked an artery. He shouldn't have been able to get back up like that. But he did, and he didn't seem too bothered about his injury. It could mean only one thing: a synth. He struggled to dislodge his right foot from a tangled mass of steel and wires.

In one deft motion, I dropped the rifle, pulled the pistol, ejected the inhibitor cartridge, loaded the EMP and took aim at his chest. It wasn't until I racked the chamber that he looked up and acknowledged my existence.

The android stood slightly shorter than me with close-cropped brown hair, and blue eyes. A perfect physique peeked out from the torn places in his shirt and chinos.

Why do they always make these robots look like marathon runners or supermodels? You never see one that looks like a tired, fat, old bus driver or one of Wagner's rotund Valkyries.

'Who are you and what the hell are you doing here?!' I barked at my quarry.

'My name is James,' the android said with a misplaced grin, 'and I could ask you the very same question. Do you make a habit of shooting random strangers?'

'Only those that jump out of the windows of abandoned buildings I happen to be standing next to,' I replied with a quick glance over my shoulder. 'Now, I'll give you one last chance to answer my question before I juice you hard enough to fry every goddamn circuit in your smug face.'

'My guess is that we are both here for the same reason.' His voice took on a slight maniacal edge. 'And that place you're thinking about shooting; you might want to hold off on that.'

He moved out of the rubble and I released the safety. That froze him in his tracks.

'There are a lot of things that I want to do, pal. And not shooting you is pretty far down on the list.'

'I assume you are here for a certain storage device with very sensitive information on it,' he replied with a shrug. 'I just thought you should know that I cached its info on my core processor. Then I smashed the original to teeny tiny bits! A jolt from your little toy might cause irreparable damage to my hardware, software or firmware. Awfully risky if you ask me!' He punctuated that last sentence with a truly insane laugh that stretched longer than one might consider appropriate. A psychotic robot. This was news, and new, to me.

Our conversation confused, and creeped, the hell out of me. I expected to find my client here waiting for me, or hiding out. Instead, this joker came flying out of the window like a deranged Peter Pan. Now he confessed that not only did he know about *the* datapad but he also had the information tucked inside his little computer heart.

Rennick had been right all along.

This shit was starting to give me another headache. I flexed my index finger against the NEEDLE's trigger and considered shooting him anyway. Better judgement won out and I tossed the cuffs to him. The android caught them with ease.

'Put them on!'

But he didn't listen to me. They never do. With a quick flick of his wrist, they came right back at me with the speed of a well-hit line drive. I dodged left, but the cuffs clipped me on the right upper arm. The hit stung but I'd been hit harder. The blow did cause me to drop my gun, though. He made a break for it to my right. I scooped up the concussion rifle and came up on one knee ready to shoot. James bolted for the gate.

I squeezed off a shot and hit him square in the ass region. It sent him airborne in a graceful arc and he crash-landed on the cracked pavement. To his credit, the robot popped right back up and kept running. I gave chase. My knee begged me not to but I ignored its protests. As fortune would have it, the handcuffs had skidded to a halt in the dirt not too far from my position. I fired again. James was at the edge of my range.

The blast knocked him down but with very little force. Still, it gave me enough time to grab the cuffs and close in. I let off another round before he could right himself and it sent him head first back onto the pockmarked concrete. I fired again and he sort of bounced on the ground but at least he stayed down. As I continued to close, I let off one more to the head for good measure.

With all the skill of a rodeo clown, I had him bound in the cuffs in no time and the low electrical pulse emitted by them kept his motor functions to a minimum. He could walk, but with the benefit of me not having to listen to his cutting wit. I pulled him to his feet and guided him to the Griffon. I opened the rear door and shoved him in the back seat.

'You sit tight, pal, and don't touch anything.'

Now to go find Charlotte Rennick.

17

I peered through the same window my back-seat passenger had made his dramatic exit from a few minutes ago and didn't really see anything of note. The main floor of the warehouse had been cleared out long ago. I did, however, see a suite of offices on a second-floor mezzanine that might contain some clues.

I opted to go in through the door. Leaping through a window seemed a little showy to me. In a few spots, giant puddles of unidentifiable liquid pooled and a thin layer of dust covered everything else. The place looked bleak and neglected. How a building in a purpose-built city some 225 million clicks from Earth could ever reach a state like this was beyond me but I'm sure it spoke volumes about the human condition. No matter where we are, no matter what far corner of the galaxy we can find to inhabit, once something has no value to us, we leave it to rot.

Upstairs wasn't much better. Wiring dangled from the false ceiling as freely as spider webs. Trash and refuse strewn about the offices suggested that they had been used, occasionally, by the homeless and hop-heads alike. I continued on – finding nothing – until I reached the supervisor's office.

Shackled to a filthy old executive chair sat an unconscious, or more likely dead, Charlotte Rennick. Her head, with her beautiful face and perfect blonde hair, leaned back against the headrest – eyes staring lifelessly at the ceiling. A pair of bracelets similar to the ones I'd used on my buddy in the car held her wrists to the armrests of the chair. Her blouse had been ripped open and a perfectly straight incision ran down her sternum between a flawless pair of breasts. The edge of the cut glistened with a substance that almost resembled blood.

'Charlotte!'

No response.

I inspected the opening more closely. Like the blood, her skin looked real but not *quite* real enough. I couldn't believe I hadn't noticed during one of our previous encounters. Gently, I pulled one of the flaps back and found the workings of a very sophisticated android. I sighed and let the piece of 'skin' go. I would have never guessed in a million years that she wasn't an actual human. Our conversation in the bar was miles apart from the banter that I had ever had with any other android, including Pam, who possessed some very human-like idiosyncrasies.

How could she not be human?

As I continued to look at her, shame and pity overcame me. Pity because I had let a client get hacked open like this. And shame because I knew then and there that I had liked Charlotte; in a more than platonic way. A lot of guys, and many ladies too, got their jollies off with synths, but not me. I preferred someone with a pulse. In my ignorance, I'd have asked her out, especially if, or when, things went south with Erica. I'd have asked her out as many times as it took to get into her pants and now I loathed myself for even thinking those thoughts.

I looked away from her and scanned the office. Some computer equipment was piled on a desk. James must have used it to transfer the information into his core processor. I also found a smashed-beyond-repair device that looked remarkably similar to the one I'd lifted from Kitterman's office. A thin layer of the same liquid that oozed out of Charlotte's chest covered it.

Instinctively, my gaze returned to my client. I had one thing left to do: take a closer look inside her chest. The delicate componentry inside her had been bashed up pretty good. I had no idea if she could ever be put back together again. If she were one of my computers, she'd be scrapped for parts.

After a few more minutes of inspection, I found the spot where the datapad had been installed. I stood back up and laughed long and hard. All this time spent chasing shadows. Putting my neck on the line. And my client had the device in her the entire time. I mean, the damned thing sat in a booth right next to me a couple of days ago. It was genius. If you wanted to keep a record of something as dangerous as the bombing in New York, then why not put it where no one would think to look?

Kitterman had brains alright, but I had the upper hand now. I had the evidence cuffed in the back seat of my car. I looked at Charlotte's lifeless body and said to her: 'Corny as it might sound, you were right all along and I'm sorry I ever doubted you.'

I closed Charlotte's blouse and jacket as best I could. She deserved a little dignity, even if she was a machine. I'd need to grab a pair of bolt cutters from my trunk to get those handcuffs off her wrists. I couldn't risk someone else finding her but I couldn't bring her with me either. A person might get the wrong idea if they saw me driving through town with a lifeless body riding shotgun and an unconscious hoodlum in the back seat.

After I had retrieved the data from my man James, I could take it, and him, to Metro HQ. Once I had spun my story to the cops, they could come back here to retrieve her body. The last thing I did before I left her was to remove the earrings and slide them into an outer pocket of my jacket.

I stood hunched over the Griffon's trunk, weapons stowed, bolt cutters in hand and back turned to the world, when an unknown assailant came at me. I heard the footsteps and had just enough time to wheel around before a guy in a ski mask could take me down with a haymaker. I dodged to my right and responded with an overhead swing of the bolt cutters.

He twisted around the attack and followed with a jab to the midsection. I reversed the direction of the bolt cutters to parry the blow. But, holy hell, this guy was strong. My counter barely phased him. He pressed his assault with a left cross that I managed to sidestep before he took my jaw off.

My sparring companion checked in around the same height and build as me. In addition to his black ski mask, he wore a baseball-style jacket, T-shirt, jeans and a pair of leather driving gloves. All in black.

The standard outfit of anyone up to no good. The only talking he did, though, was with his fists and they had a lot to say.

He came at me again with another left. I deflected most of the blow, but it still hurt like a son of a bitch. I swung the cutters again. He flowed past them like a leaf rustling in the wind and chopped my wrist, forcing them loose from my grip. They fell at our feet with a loud clang. At this point, I knew I was in it deep and didn't see a way out of this fight. I prayed to God that Ski Mask wasn't entertaining any homicidal notions.

Unnoticed, I reached into my pocket and palmed the earrings. They might come in handy if I survived the fight. This guy didn't show up, mitts swinging and nothing to say, by accident. He showed up for the same reason I did. Charlotte Rennick.

The trail of crumbs all led back to her. Not to me. But to her.

My attacker let fly an uppercut with his right. I closed the distance to trap the punch with my left arm and practically hugged the guy. We stood there face to face. His breath was even and calm. An obvious sign that this pug could go the distance with a better opponent. I did the only thing I could do: I lunged forward, my cranium leading the charge. At the same time as I attempted to headbutt my opponent, I slipped the earrings in his jacket pocket. The drop went perfectly. However, when our foreheads met, it felt more like hitting a brick wall than someone's skull. Stars flashed in my vision and my knees buckled.

In my moment of disorientation, the guy paid me back in kind with his own head-to-head strike and absolutely stunned me. He followed with a knee to the midsection and then a right elbow to the head. He finished his flurry of blows with a left jab straight at my already tenderised forehead with a force so hard that it sent me staggering backwards. He pressed the attack.

I fought to maintain consciousness and flailed at him like a drunken sailor. I missed a lot, but by some miracle my fingers hooked the eye holes of his ski mask. I wrenched it off as I continued to stumble backwards. Darkness closed in all around me. He followed with another right to the chest and oblivion swelled up around me.

My opponent stopped moving just long enough for me to get a good look at him. A face I'd seen before. I had seen it recently. I knew that face. I also knew my eyes must've been playing tricks on me. Because the mug I saw as the shadows claimed me was none other than Nolan Kitterman.

18

Slowly, the conscious world manifested itself as a tiny beam of light. As the light expanded, a voice telling me to *get up* joined in the fun. I decided, what the hell, I might as well listen and opened my eyes. Immediately I regretted it because with consciousness came pain. Pain in my chest. Pain in my jaw and forehead. Pain in my arms and hands. Pain everywhere.

I shielded my eyes with my right hand and massaged my temples with my middle finger and thumb.

'Maybe I should go back to practising law,' I groaned and continued to lie there.

After a few minutes of self-pity, I leaned up on my elbows and had a look around through squinted eyes. No sign of the guy or his ski mask. He must have bolted while I snoozed like a baby. My car, fortunately, hadn't disappeared, and I counted it as a blessing. But the opened rear passenger door sat on its hinges in an odd sort of way. Out of the back seat lay the sprawling figure of James with most of his electronic guts dangling on the pavement.

I sat up and regretted that, too. The ache in my head increased tenfold. The world around me faded in and out of focus. Details split in two and migrated in opposite directions before converging into one again. I fought through it, managed to roll over on my hands and knees, and crawl over to the dead robot for a closer inspection. Now, I'm no android expert but if I had to guess, I would say the punk who bushwhacked me went for this guy's core processor.

There went the evidence against Kitterman.

I dropped onto my keister, leaned back against the car next to the lifeless high-tech tin can and tried to get my bearings. I needed to think for a few minutes and, in all fairness, couldn't do more than that anyway. Anything else hurt too much. I checked the time… Out at least 40 minutes. Looking at my smartwatch reminded me that I had dropped those earrings into Ski Mask's pocket during the fight. I opened the tracking application and waited for it to acquire the signal. He was on the Underground, heading towards RD1 from Res 3. I watched the dot, transfixed, waiting to see where he would go next but it went dead. 'Signal Lost' flashed on the screen. He must've found the earrings and smashed them.

RD1.

MARA Corp. Kitterman.

The image of her old man flashed in my mind for reasons that momentarily eluded me. Then it hit me: I saw his face before I blacked out. A dead man had punched me out. And where there was one Kitterman involved, there stood a very good chance to find another.

'What do you make of that?' I said to the silent companion lying next to me.

He didn't respond.

I laughed.

It was all I had in me; to sit there and laugh. It felt good despite the tenderness in my chest and sides. I needed a nice, hearty laugh. When the hilarity of the situation died down, I hauled myself up to a standing position, fighting off the nausea along the way.

A few slow deep breaths and I started to feel on the right side of 'better'. I went around the mechanical corpse and had a closer look at the car door. The damage hadn't been too extensive and it could be closed if there wasn't a body in the way. The Griffon would need some TLC but it'd be alright in the end. That cheered me up a bit more.

I turned my attention to the empty building where I hoped Rennick's body still lay. No way in hell a third dude would be lurking around here waiting to beat my ass, but that didn't change the fact that the dump looked even more foreboding than ever. For peace of mind, I grabbed my concussion rifle and staggered towards the same rusty door I had used an hour ago.

The place looked exactly the same. No one had entered since I left, as far as I could tell. Upstairs I found Ms Rennick precisely where I had stashed her. Ski Mask had left both me and her alone. I guess he was only after one thing.

I stumbled my way back to the car and opened the secret compartment. I stashed the rifle and the pistol and the extra cartridge in the space. Next, I scrolled through the list of contacts on my smartwatch until I found Detective Ashdown's number again. I had to call this one in to Metro because I couldn't hide my involvement in what went down at Verne Bottling. Two dead androids and a shoddy excuse for being here already put me at a disadvantage. Not to mention, Rennick worked for Kitterman, and I had broken into her place. Another crumb that could lead back to me.

Ashdown's voice brought me out of my head.

'Daniel Helmqvist. What can I do for you today?'

His hello was about as warm as a bank teller's.

'I'd hate for you to detect a pattern in our recent phone conversations, but…' I took a deep breath. 'You better send some boys down to the IM. I've got two dead androids at the old Verne factory.'

'Dead?'

'Dead, disabled, guts hanging out. Call it what you want but they ain't hosting tea parties any time soon.'

'What the hell are you mixed up in this time, Helm?'

Still no real concern in his voice, only the curiosity of someone used to solving mysteries.

'I'll tell you when you get here.'

'Fine. We're on our way. The old Verne plant, you say?'

'Yeah. 1643 Edison.'

'Got it. We'll be there in twenty. Don't go anywhere.'

'I wouldn't dream of it. You boys showing up with sirens blazing will be the highlight of my day.'

'Are you in danger?'

'Not anymore.'

'No sirens then.'

'You really know how to take the fun out of everything, don't you?'

He hung up on me.

Before I hopped into the driver's seat to await the arrival of Metro I realised I'd made a mistake by stowing away the concussion rifle. The gun would have to figure into my story and I owned a permit for it anyway. The NEEDLE, however, had to be hidden. I didn't use it and after what happened in the HTS case, Ashdown wouldn't let this one slide.

I placed the rifle on the hood of the car so as to not make anyone with an actual firearm jumpy when they saw it. The coppers rolling up to a scene in their cruisers and spying some gee with a gun hitched up on his shoulder like a cowboy might send the wrong message. With the stage set, I slid in behind the steering wheel and powered up the car to access the on-board computer. From there, I locked the hidden compartment in the trunk. And, at the same time, scrolled through my music collection for something to listen to while I waited. I settled on Bonobo's *The North Borders*.

About 25 minutes after I had spoken to Ashdown, he delivered on his promise. A squad car and an unmarked cruiser came through the gate of the Verne Bottling Company.

No sirens.

No lights.

Nothing.

I shut the music off and pulled myself out of the car. I still felt like I had gone whitewater rafting without a boat but the pain had subsided somewhat. Or maybe I was just getting used to it.

Ashdown, and another detective I didn't recognise, climbed out of the unmarked cruiser. Out of the other car came two uniformed policemen. No coroner. No ME. No forensic unit. Like I said, no one really cared about how and when a robot bit it.

Ash strolled up to me and regarded me with suspicion. 'You mentioned two dead on the phone, but left out the part where one was hanging out of your back seat. Care to enlighten me?'

I shifted my gaze over to his minions as they inspected the lifeless robot dangling out of my car. 'I happened to be in the area. I heard a scream and I stopped to investigate. I entered through the hole you boys just came through and grabbed my concussion rifle.' I jerked my thumb in its direction. Ashdown's eyes drifted from me to it. I kept talking.

'I went up to the building to get a closer look and then a guy comes flying through that broken window.'

I stopped, turned and pointed to the jagged pane of glass. Ashdown walked over to it. I followed.

'Where were you?' he asked without looking at me.

'Over by that door. I told him to halt but he came at me. I let off one round into his chest and sent him into that scrap heap over there.'

'Did you know he was a synthetic at the time?'

'No, not until he extracted himself from the pile.'

The detective wrote a few things down on a Mini MIX5, or mMIX5, with a stylus. 'At that point, what made you realise he was an android?'

'The way he didn't bleed, he should've been in a bad way. Instead, he took off running like he had missed the bus.'

'Did he say anything to you?'

'No,' I lied.

'He attacked you and when that didn't work out too well for him, he tried to make a break for it? Is that what you're telling me?'

'That's exactly what I'm telling you, John.'

'How did you subdue him?' he replied as he turned his attention from the notepad to the mound of junk in question.

'I shot him again in the back. That sent him flying. I closed the gap and hit him again with a disabling blast. That allowed me to cuff him.'

'Good thing you had that rifle on ya, Helm.'

That was more than a kindly statement of fact.

'I have a permit for it.'

'Great. Would you like to show it to me?'

I pulled out a billfold with a PI's badge on one flap and a small smart-glass screen with all my licensing details on the other.

He scrolled through my information like he was looking through a Burberry catalogue and then handed them back to me.

'You said that you heard a scream. Where did it come from?'

'Inside the factory.'

'Did you check it out?'

'Yeah, after I had the male robot secured in the back seat.'

'What did you find?'

'Let me show you.'

I took him in and up to where I had stashed Charlotte Rennick's body. He looked the scene over – careful not to touch anything – and then inspected her more closely.

'So you don't know the victim?' he asked me, still looking at the place where Charlotte's chest had been ripped open, pulling a flap of skin back with his stylus.

'Never seen her before in my life.'

More lies. Layer after layer of lies stacked like a house of cards waiting for the right breeze to come along and send it tumbling to the ground. It wouldn't be too difficult to prove I knew Charlotte. I had to gamble, however, on the fact that this incident wouldn't go very far. An inspection of the componentry within Rennick's body, or into her life, would undoubtedly lead to her connection to MARA Corporation. What James had confessed to me. What happened to James after he told me his secret. The dude who had knocked me out bearing a strong resemblance to Nolan Kitterman. They would undoubtedly lead an investigation straight to Kitterman. She couldn't let that happen. Rich people like her almost always had politicians in their pocket. She would use them to make this go away. If I played this right, I'd escape any trouble as well. Trouble from the police, at any rate.

He motioned to the door and we left the building.

'And you just happened to be driving by and heard a scream?' he asked me again once we were outside.

'That's right. Some timing, eh?' I replied, trying to gauge his reaction.

'Almost hard to believe, Helm. What were you doing in the area?'

'I was thinking about getting some lunch at the 3rd Street.'

'Curt has a menu now?'

'I didn't know you frequented the Lounge.'

'I don't.'

'Then how do you know who owns it?'

'It's my business to know things.'

'Of course, you're a damn good detective,' I responded with false deference. 'Anyway, no, they don't serve food. I had a liquid lunch in mind.'

'So let me get this straight, you're in the area on an afternoon drive through the picturesque IM, happen upon a crime in progress, take matters into your own hands, and apprehend this guy,' he said as he returned to the subject at hand.

'To a tee. If you type that up on your mini MIX, I'll sign it and we can all be on our merry way.'

'I'd love to Helm 'cept there's just one problem. The guy you bagged is pulled to pieces all over your back seat. Wanna tell me about that?'

'As soon as I had the perp secured, another assailant ambushed me. We struggled but he laid me out pretty good.'

'This second guy got the jump on you?'

'Mmhhmm. He came at me from behind. I had just enough time to defend myself.'

'By defend yourself, do you mean get beaten until you were unconscious?'

'How did you guess?'

'You look like shit.'

I ran a hand over my cheeks and jaw. 'Pretty obvious, huh?'

He nodded this time.

'When I came to, I found the scene like this and called you guys.'

'Why didn't you call when you first arrived? I can never understand why types like you always have to play the hero. First Berkshire. And now this?' His tone thick with accusation.

'Hey! I was working a case the other day and it turned violent. I did what I did today because I thought a woman was in trouble. Anyway, you, of all people, should know better than to call me a hero.'

'So you knew that it was a woman? You said you'd never seen her before.'

Clever, Ash. Trying to trip me up like that.

'Maybe I misspoke in the beginning. I distinctly heard a woman's voice when I stopped to investigate.'

That gave him a moment's pause.

'You still should have called the police. This is what we do. This is our job. Not some gumshoe's with a strong sense of civic duty.'

'He would have gotten away.'

Ashdown walked over to the mechanical corpse and bent down to look at it closer. 'Yeah, well, he's a lot of use to us now. Thanks.'

'Screw you, John. I followed my instincts. If you don't like it, then too bad. What's done is done. How was I supposed to know another guy was lurking in the shadows?'

'Fine,' the detective said with a sigh. 'I know you mean well, but, look, this whole thing is fishy. We have two androids with their guts ripped out and a third person on the loose. Did you get a look at this other guy?'

I shook my head. 'Sorry, he had a mask on.'

'Naturally,' Ashdown replied unkindly. Silence descended upon the scene as the detective looked around for a few more minutes. Everyone else fidgeted, waiting for the next move.

'I'm going to need you to come into the station, Helm,' he said at last. 'We'll need you to sign another statement.'

'I figured as much. What about the robots?'

'Fernie and Ross'll take care of them.' He motioned to the two beat cops and they joined us.

'There is another synthetic in an office on the mezzanine of the bottling factory,' the detective said to them. 'Bring her down and load her, along with the one in Helm's car, into a forensic bus once it arrives. On my way back to RD1, I'll put a call in for a CSI unit to process this place.'

Normally moving bodies around before forensics showed up would never fly. You don't mess with a crime scene like that but it's always a tad different when androids are involved. They don't get the same treatment as an actual person.

'Can I take my car?' I asked with misplaced optimism.

'Sorry, but we need to dust it for prints and what not. My boys'll guard it until a tow truck arrives. When lab's done with it, we'll get back to you.'

'I'd like to stay here until your guys are finished with it. If that's alright.'

'Why do you want to keep an eye on it, Helm? Afraid of what we might find?'

'Quite the opposite,' I replied casually. 'This is my baby and a pretty rare one at that. I'd hate to see it mishandled.'

Ashdown turned his options over in his mind.

'Alright, stay here if you want but once they're done with your car, go straight to HQ. Got it? No stopping anywhere. If you do, we'll know. We know everything.'

'Thanks.' I extended my hand as a friendly gesture. He looked at it, stuffed his hands in his pockets, turned and strolled back to his car.

'No stops,' he called out over the unmarked cruiser's doorframe as he slid into the passenger seat. His partner started the engine, and they left me in a cloud of dust with the two beat cops.

Ross and Fernie cast a wary glance at me, not knowing whether they should leave me alone long enough to grab Rennick's body.

'Don't worry, fellas,' I said as I leaned on the hood of the Griffon. 'I'm not going anywhere.'

19

It didn't take crime scene investigators very long to arrive at the abandoned factory. Once there, they dusted for prints and swept for any organic matter from which they could salvage a DNA sample. They went through the passenger cabin, and checked under the hood. I presented the best picture of calm I could by focusing on the tumbler of gin I'd destroy at the first opportunity.

When they moved to the trunk, my heart picked up its pace to a quick beat. I didn't figure they'd find my secret hidey-hole but you never know with these lab techs. One in a million actually cares about doing a good job. If they noticed me hovering around when they popped the trunk, they didn't let on. And they didn't find anything out of the ordinary either. Eventually, they let me leave – with my car. The lead agent reminded me to proceed directly to Metro HQ.

The damaged rear door wouldn't shut properly, and my insistence on driving it away from the scene should've been a warning sign to them. Nonetheless, I forged ahead and told the agent I'd have to drop my car off at a garage called Theo's Hi-Tech Automotive. Afterwards, I'd take a cab straight to the police station. I gave the guy the address and phone number of Theo's garage. He advised me against it and I promptly ignored him.

I put the passenger side windows down and lashed my belt around the frames of the front and rear doors. It wasn't exactly street legal, but desperate times and all that. The head police nerd watched for a moment, shook his head and went back to work. As I left the lot, I could see him placing a call. I had no doubts who'd be picking up on the other end.

Driving with the windows down on one side of the car was a strange experience because I can't think of a time when I had ever driven with any of the windows down. The sounds of the world around me filled the cabin. I felt connected to the city and a little less weary from the beating I had taken back in the IM.

The trip to Theo's shop in the Commercial District also gave me time to mull a few things over. I had an idea about how to proceed in the case, assuming I survived another encounter with Ashdown on his home turf. But my current little stunt wasn't going to help matters. The detective had extended me a huge courtesy by letting me keep my car and I was doing a pretty poor job of showing my appreciation.

Ah well, I couldn't let them take the car in for processing. Sooner or later, they would have found all my dirty little secrets. It was worth a shot to see if the detective would let me drive the car to the police station. And it worked.

By the time I had turned all this over in my mind, I had entered the CD and was minutes away from one of the best mechanics in all of New London. I parked in the first available spot and went through a door marked 'Customers'. There behind the counter typing something into a computer stood Theo.

Theo had me beat in height, weight, kindness and human decency. He wore a crazy afro, a wild beard to match, and a perpetual smile. In his one-piece, green mechanics suit he could only be described as 'jolly'. He reminded me of one of the Cheeryble brothers come to life.

Theo once told me that his family had immigrated to here from Senegal after a short stint in Manchester, England. His parents had sold everything they owned in a bold attempt to move to New London and open a North African restaurant. They had been reasonably successful restaurant/night club owners back on Earth and thought that Mars might give them the opportunity for the sort of financial success that they never had in Senegal or one of the largest cities in Britain.

Yep, New London had supplanted America as the 'land of opportunity' and those who could afford it came here. Unfortunately, the restaurant failed and Theo's father, Theo Sr, fell back on the only other thing that he was skilled at – fixing cars. Theo Jr inherited the business a little over a decade ago and has been here ever since.

I met Theo by pure happenstance. A lifetime ago, he supplied testimony in a murder case that had fallen into my lap. He struck me as an earnest man and helped make a conviction for the prosecution.

It wasn't until a couple of years after the trial, when I had taken up the PI racket, that I learned just how devious he could be. And I am the better man for it.

The first time I took the Griffon to his shop for a service check-up he suggested that he could make a few modifications to it that might come in handy. It was his idea for the compartment in the trunk 'because you never know what a private eye might need to hide'. He designed it, installed it and I helped him programme the security features. Today was the first real test and it passed with flying colours. I owed Theo big time.

When I walked in, his usually bright smile faltered.

'You don't look so good.'

'Thanks. I don't feel too great, either, if it helps. A dust up over in IM, but, hey, I don't have a whole lot of time. Metro is expecting me in RD1.'

He nodded and put on his business face. But those eyes of his – I don't think he could ever look too serious. 'Why'd you come here then?'

'The Griffon has a few minor dings that need repairing.'

'Minor dings?'

'Yeah, the rear passenger door is a bit screwy. Can you fix it?'

We stepped out to the parking lot. While Theo busied himself with surveying the damage, I called for a cab. He gave me an estimate and an idea of how long it'd take to fix the car. I told him to take his time and to maybe leave the special compartment alone.

'I told you it would come in handy,' he laughed and I knew my secret would be safe with him.

20

Only the MARA Corporation executive building eclipsed Metro HQ as the tallest in the RD1. By Earth standards, a premise with only six floors wasn't much to write home about. Then again, the sky is the limit on Earth. But not here. Not in a world encased in domes. Anyway, something doesn't need to be 150 storeys high to be impressive. Just ask the Pope.

The design of the edifice is loosely based on the head office of Scotland Yard completed in 2015. In that way, New London's Metro HQ building follows many of the Neo-Classical forms of the original, but with one major modification. The walls of the ground floor are made from crystal-clear glass panes. It gives the appearance that the rest of the structure is floating above the ground. The elevators and staircases connect the ground floor to the rest of the building, making it look like something out of an Escher lithograph.

I walked in the front door, approached the on-duty desk, gave my name and why I was there. The policewoman manning the station made a phone call and then waved me off to a row of chairs. It didn't take very long. A uniformed officer appeared within five minutes and escorted me up to the detectives' bullpen of the third floor. I tried to see if I could spot Ashdown but he was nowhere to be found. My taciturn chaperone deposited me into an interrogation room.

From the manner in which I shifted around in my seat, any-one watching from the video feed or on the other side of the mirror may have thought the pressure had gotten to me. That I had something to hide. Truth of it, though, was I hurt. I'd been worked over pretty good and they didn't have comfort in mind when they furnished these rooms. All I wanted to do was go home. Eventually, the detective graced me with his presence.

'Glad to see you didn't forget about me,' I said with very little kindness as he sat down.

'Spare me your indignation, Helm. You made me look like a chump by not coming straight here.'

He placed a MIX11 between us – its blank screen reflected the ceiling lights – and continued.

'What's in the car?'

'What do you mean?' I can play 20 Questions, too.

He sighed. 'You seemed a tad antsy back at the scene but I wanted to give you the benefit of the doubt. Now I'm thinkin' I should've hauled your ass down here in the back of my cruiser. So again, I ask what's in the car?'

'Nothing. Your field techs went through it pretty thoroughly, John—' He cut me off.

'Right now, it's Detective Ashdown.'

'Anyway, like I said, *Detective*, they went over the entire car with a fine tooth comb and they didn't find anything suspicious. But I suspect they already told you that. I don't have anything to hide except an irrational love affair with a car. Sue me if you've got a problem with me wanting to get it fixed up as soon as possible.'

'Maybe not sue you, Helm, but I'm sure that we could get some obstruction charges levelled against you,' he replied, and then stopped short. I don't think he wanted to get into a shouting match. 'Don't tread on any more favours I do for you, Helm.'

'Yeah, sorry,' I said, starting to feel like an ass. 'Is that all? Another statement to sign on your tablet?'

'Where were you Saturday night?'

The question caught me off guard and I just looked at him for a moment.

'Saturday night,' he repeated.

'Out on a date. We went to DKY for dinner and then back to my place.'

'You were at your place the entire night, then?'

He gave me a cold hard stare. I felt like I was sitting in front of my dad, getting a telling off. The anger that had somewhat abated flared up again. I crossed my arms defensively and I noted the faintest glimmer of a smile pull at the corner of his lips.

If I was a lesser soul – and by that I mean someone not used to a cross-examination – he would have had me dead to rights. He was playing me pretty good and I'd say that within five minutes I'd have said something that I shouldn't have said. Fortunately, I knew my way around this game as well as he did. I kept up my defensive posture but tried to use it to my advantage.

'Yeah, I was at home the entire night. My date can confirm it. Her name is Erica Green. I don't have her number off the top of my head, but she lives at 422 West Willis, Res 2.'

Ashdown glanced up at a video camera and then back to me. A signal to check her out. Erica was going to get dragged into this. Time to see if she could sell a lie to a veteran member of Metro Police. I had my doubts and in the process lost all sense of reason.

'What's this all about? Is it about the break-in at MARA Corp late Saturday/early Sunday?'

'Who said anything about a break-in?' He tensed because he smelled a mistake on my part. I turned up the crazy.

'MNN reported the break-in into a "high-tech facility".'

'There are a lot of high-tech facilities in this city, Helm.'

'Not a lot with a security team swarming around them on Sunday like a pack of determined bloodhounds. It doesn't take genius-level deductive skills to make the connection. Anyway, why are you asking me about Saturday in a very accusatory manner? The article said an arrest had been made.'

'Because someone smarter than the half-wit we scooped up last night *did* have something to do with the break-in, that's for sure. The job was way too sophisticated for him and there aren't a whole lot of people with the type of training required to infiltrate a facility such as MARA Corporation undetected.' He leaned back in his chair with the MIX in hand. The glow from the screen reflected off his face. 'But you do from your service days.'

'Was anything taken?' I asked trying to deflect the conversation away from me.

'No,' he answered, without conviction.

'So if that's the case, then was he caught trying to break into MARA Corp? I ask because I'm trying to understand why you arrested a man you don't think is connected to the break-in.'

Ashdown waffled. He couldn't lie here because the news article said the arrest happened this morning, and I already established that I had read it.

'Fine,' the detective replied on the back end of a sigh. 'The perp was found in possession of stolen goods from MARA Corp.'

I crossed my arms. 'I don't understand why you're asking me where I was, and what I was doing last night. Whether you believe it, or not, you have your guy. Seems to me like an open-and-shut case.'

'Because the guy insisted that he found the stolen property in an alley in Res 3. And, like I said, he isn't exactly the criminal mastermind type. He isn't lying. I've been in this business long enough to know when I'm being lied to.'

'Has he named any accomplices?'

'No. He's sticking to his story about finding the item in question in the alley. The guy has no record. No reason to lie. I think someone put it there, and he found it.'

I shook my head and affected a chuckle. All part of the show.

'So let me get this straight. You think that I busted into MARA Corp, boosted some item from inside the building, then dumped it in an alley for some poor slob to stumble across and take the heat for me? Why would I even do that? Risk a b-and-e, then further risk getting caught by disposing of it in an alley? Why not destroy it? Or hide it for no one to ever find? I'd like to think I'm smarter than that.'

'It's hard to say what you would do, Helm. Maybe you didn't like what you found. Maybe someone hired you to do it to send a message to Kitterman that her joint isn't as secure as she might think it is. It could be a hundred different things. But what I do know is that we have video of you driving through Res 3 yesterday and then you were in the area today. It's all a bit suspicious, even you have to admit that.'

'I bet that you have video of me driving through a lot of places, yesterday. In fact, if you review the files long enough, you'll see me staggering out of the 3rd Street Lounge after midnight. Maybe I just have a soft spot for the worst parts of this town. Anyway, John, do you have actual video of me getting out of my car and disposing of the item? Or any other evidence to connect me to it? Do you have anything that isn't circumstantial?' I had used his first name, again, to try to rile him up a bit and throw him off his game.

He didn't rise to the bait and continued to look at me through narrowed eyes. I figured I might as well keep talking.

'As for why I was in the area yesterday, I was out for a drive, and I like to visit the old neighbourhood from time to time. Last time I checked, that isn't a crime. And you already know why I was on the east side today. I made a statement, which is why I thought you called me down here – to sign it.'

Now to apply a little righteous indignation to the situation: I put my hands on the table and leaned in for the full effect.

'Not to mention, that if you had anything solid on me,' I continued, raising my voice just a tad, 'you wouldn't have let me take my car today. You would have brought me in yourself. These accusations you're trying to hang on me are all last minute and I don't know what you're playing at, Detective, but it stinks.'

'Calm down, Helm, they're routine. That's all.'

He eyed me again warily. 'No need to get worked up into a huff. You are one of the few people that could pull off a heist like that and you know that you are. I'd be a piss-poor cop if I didn't question you – and you know that too.'

A light flashed on the wall and Ashdown stood up. 'I'll be back shortly.'

With his MIX11 in hand, he made for the door.

'Can I at least get a cup of Joe while I wait?'

'Sure. I'll have one of the uniforms bring you one. In the meantime, sit tight.' He walked out and left me alone, again, with my thoughts.

A couple of minutes later a beat cop brought me a paper cup filled with slightly-warmer-than-room-temperature coffee. Under normal circumstances, I wouldn't have touched it. But these weren't normal circumstances and the act of drinking it gave me something to do.

Nothing but cold dregs remained when the detective returned to my interrogation room. He pushed his tablet and a stylus in front of me. My statement from today filled the display.

'I'm guessing my alibi checks out,' I said as I looked down at the document.

'Yeah, Ms Green confirmed your story and we have no evidence of you leaving your place. It must've been someone else.'

Whew! I owed her big time now.

The statement appeared to be on the up-and-up so I autographed it and pushed it back towards Ashdown's side of the table.

'Am I free to leave?'

He picked up the computer, glanced at the signature line, and put it to sleep.

'You're free to go.'

I stood and walked out of the room.

'Look, no hard feelings,' he said as I passed him at the doorway. 'I'm just doing my job and chasing leads. You know how it is.'

I scanned the area quickly and saw Erica being led out of the bullpen by another police officer. She looked good. I kept quiet as I watched her head to the elevator bank. I wasn't sure how I could thank her and hoped she might have a suggestion or two.

'Sure, John, no hard feelings,' I replied with a distinct lack of sincerity as I looked back at Ashdown.

'Juarez'll take you downstairs.' He extended a hand to shake.

I pulled a move from his playbook and jammed my hands into my pockets and followed Juarez towards the elevator bank.

21

On the main floor, the desk officer, a guy this time, signed me out. By the time I was a free man, I spied Erica walking towards the subway entrance. I dashed out of the building and called her name.

'Erica!'

She turned back. A smile that was equal parts relief and happiness seemed to spread on her face. We met and hugged.

'Thanks for the alibi.'

'I'm not saying I'd like to make a habit out of it, but if it helped keep you a free man, then all the better.'

'How did it go?'

'Well enough, I suppose. We're both here, right?'

'True. Sorry about that. You came up during an interview.'

'About the other night?'

People flowed past us on the sidewalk like leaves on a lazy river.

'Not at first, no. The interview started out as this' – I swirled my hand around my face to highlight the areas I'd been punched – 'and turned into the other night.'

She had to know what the other night was about. She read the news. She's smart. I admired her resolve to help me out even more.

A look of concern crossed her features.

'Are you okay?'

'More or less. I think.'

Erica checked her smartwatch. 'Listen, can we walk and talk? I'm late for work.'

Thrown off, I checked my own MAX. 'Can we meet later? I need to see about my car and a few other things.'

'Is one of them a trip to the doctor's office?'

'It might be.'

'Sure, Danny.' She touched my bruised cheek. 'Call me later?'

'Definitely.'

With that, Erica turned and walked towards the escalator down to the Underground station. I scanned the streets for an available cab.

The arrival of a stretch Baker Electric hijacked my attempt to hail an approaching LTI. A guy in a well-cut suit and trench coat, who looked like he could be the starting linebacker on any pro team, climbed out.

'Daniel Helmqvist?' he asked with a clear powerful voice and approached me.

'It depends on who's asking,' I replied and almost immediately regretted it.

He grabbed me by the upper arm with fingers like a vice grip.

'A real jokester, eh? Come on. Someone wants to see you.'

He then proceeded to walk me to the limo whether I wanted to or not.

'Easy, pal,' I said. 'We're in front of Metro HQ. I call out and you've got a ton of heat on you in the blink of an eye.'

He relaxed a bit and looked around as if he only now realised where we were. 'Get in the car.'

I slid into an open space on the left side of the rear compartment. On the bench seat opposite me were two other passengers. The linebacker hopped into the space closest to the door. The car immediately merged into traffic.

The meathead sitting to my left looked to be cut from the same cloth as the one who ushered me into this luxury carriage. Together they presented a formidable pair of bruisers. I knew without hesitation that these guys took great delight in working over somebody. Sandwiched between the two pillars of muscle sat a woman of modest beauty. She had a soft chin, high cheekbones and a Roman nose. Her shoulder-length hair was a deep chestnut brown. She wore a pencil-skirt suit and that bored look popular amongst the super smart.

'Ms Kitterman, what a pleasant surprise,' I said with a slight smile and quick survey of the Baker. 'This definitely beats your run-of-the-mill taxi crawling around New London but I suspect that you aren't here to give me a lift back to my office, are you?'

The guy to her left clenched his right hand into a tight fist. Without turning her gaze from me, she patted his arm. He relaxed it a bit.

'I have heard that you have quite the sense of humour, Mr Helmqvist,' she replied with a soft voice that still retained a trace of Northern Ireland. 'I thought that it was the least I could do as a thank you for the safe return of my property.'

Her ambiguity put me on edge. I all but gulped. Property? Was this about Sunday morning? Or something else related to today? The best course of action was to play dumb.

'I don't follow,' I said after some hesitation.

She adjusted herself in her seat slightly, fixing her skirt as she did so.

'I was led to believe you found my android in an abandoned warehouse today and telephoned the police.'

At that precise moment, I noticed her eyes for the first time. Deep emerald green, nearly the same shade and shape as Charlotte Rennick's. Mara must have modelled the android after herself. The differences in face and body spoke volumes as to how Kitterman must've viewed herself. But the eyes... Who could forget those?

If we all had a chance to play God, I suppose we'd all make ourselves in our own image. It also explained why Mara would keep the datapad inside my client. I guess, though, Mara never underestimated the steadfast loyalty of her creation. A story as old as time. But at least she didn't name her Eve.

'It was no trouble at all, Ms Kitterman. I just happened to be in the right place at the right time.'

Not unlike her pulling up moments after I parted ways with Ashdown. Coincidence? Hardly, but I didn't peg the detective as some two-bit stoolie on Kitterman's payroll. It had to be someone else but the list of potentials was too long to devote a whole lot of mental energy to it. Kitterman had me in her ride for one reason: information. What did I know and what did I tell the police?

'Anyway, there was no need to collect me from the police station,' I continued. 'If you wanted to thank me, you could've called my office or paid me a visit there in person.' I reached for the door handle. 'Now, if you'd be so kind as to tell the driver to stop, I'll get out here.'

This time the goon to my right roughly pushed me back into my seat.

I gave the thug a hard look but he wasn't impressed. 'Or not.'

'Don't be so discourteous, Mr Helmqvist,' Mara said with that patronising voice that all wealthy Brits seem to have at their disposal.

'Me?' I said with genuine disbelief. 'I'm not the one taking a guy on a sightseeing tour of New London against his will.' And a tour it was. We'd left RD1 by way of the tunnel that connected it to the IM but turned right at the Inner Ring road. The plan seemed to be to drive as many orbits around the district as it took to satisfy Kitterman's curiosity.

Anyway, that last comment didn't go over so well. She unleashed bodyguard No. 2 on my left, with nothing more than a furtive glance his way. He leaned over and backhanded me on the right side of my face. It was like getting hit with a frying pan.

'I'd say something about you proving my point, but I think that I'd just get more of the same,' I finished as I rubbed my jaw.

'Now, now, Mr Helmqvist. Don't be so dramatic, and I would suggest dropping the attitude. I would hate to see your face bruised any more than it already is.'

I slumped into my seat. 'Fine. What do you want from me?'

'I would like to know what happened today. That is all.'

'What's there to tell? I already gave the police my statement and I'm sure that you've already seen it.'

She arched her eyebrow questioningly. I knew my mouth was going to get me in trouble but it didn't stop me from asking for more of the rough stuff.

'Oh, come on! I suppose that you just happened to be passing by the police station and it suddenly occurred to you that I might need a lift. We both know that you knew exactly when I was being released.'

'Are you suggesting that I have informants in the police department?'

'Yeah, pretty much.' This time the thug on my right leaned in and landed a solid blow to my chest. It threw me into a coughing fit. He leaned back and admired his handy work.

'We do not have to do it this way, Mr Helmqvist. I am simply trying to learn all that I can about the attack on my employee today,' Mara said once I finished hacking my lungs out.

'You mean the robot?'

'Android, yes, but Charlotte was very dear to me and I like to think of her as more than a soulless machine.'

'Such devotion to your creation. How touching. A regular Doctor Frankenstein.' A fiery glow sparked in the depths of her eyes and her nostrils flared in anger.

'Such impertinence,' she said with a voice dripping with venom. The comment earned me a love tap to the chest again by both goons. I started coughing again. Flecks of blood hit my hand as I covered my mouth. Once I regained some of my composure, I chuckled.

'Is this how you win people over, Kitterman? Beat the hell out of them until they tell you what you want?'

'Not usually, no. However, in cases where my guest proves difficult then, I am afraid to say, much more physical measures must be taken. You really should be more forthcoming when I ask you a question.'

'Well, this approach doesn't inspire cooperation. I'll give you that one for free.' I took a handkerchief out of my pocket and dabbed the blood away from my mouth.

'You would be surprised at its efficiency. Now about today. What did you tell the police?'

'Nothing,' I replied, with an attempt at mock injury that probably looked like real injury. 'I heard a scream. I pulled up, encountered the assailant who identified himself as James, incapacitated him, found your android, and then got KO'd by someone else.'

'So you just *happened* to arrive at an abandoned warehouse in an isolated part of town? You weren't following Charlotte or had some means of tracking her?'

'Why would I have a tracking device on an android that I never met before?'

'We have reason to think otherwise.'

By 'we' she meant 'she', no doubt about that. She must have been told about the earrings. This little morsel of information confirmed my belief that the guy who knocked me out and Mara Kitterman were connected. If she admitted knowledge of the earrings, she'd reveal that connection. I thought I would roll the dice and see what happened.

'That's nice. Really it is. But can you prove I had encountered your robot before today?'

'Unfortunately, no.'

She held her breath slightly when she said that. A lie. It had to be, and spoke volumes as to her willingness to protect her relationship with a guy who looked like her dead father. Nevertheless, her response gave me the confidence to push my own lie a little further.

'Like I said, I've never seen her before in my life.'

She narrowed her eyes again and I braced for impact. Instead, she checked her smartwatch – a **MAX** model I'd not yet seen – and then adjusted her suit jacket.

We drove in silence for a few minutes. I looked out the window and could make out the Res 1 dome on our left. Kitterman simply stared at me, waiting for me to spill the beans. I knew I needed to say something to escape her clutches.

'Look,' I said after I cleared my throat, 'the only thing I can add to the conversation is that it looked like the James character had torn something out of your android – most likely a storage device. Then, if I am right, he transferred the information to an internal storage device that was later ripped out by the party-crasher. But I suspect that you knew that already.'

Her eyes narrowed and the two punks flanking her tensed again like coiled springs. I prepared for the worst but then she relaxed. As if on cue, the two guys did the same.

'What's that supposed to mean?'

'That you've probably already got the female back in your lab and have seen the extent of the damage. Plus, since she is your property, whatever was inside of her, you put it there. I think what you *should* have asked me all along, Ms Kitterman is: "at any point did you look at the information on the storage device that was forcibly taken out of Ms Rennick?" To which I would answer, no.'

She laughed. It was – and I hate to admit this – a very charming laugh.

'Perhaps you are right, Mr Helmqvist. Perhaps I shouldn't have been so enigmatic with my intentions today.' She paused and whispered something to the driver. At the next roundabout, I glanced out the window and saw that we turned right again. We were heading back to RD1. I might just make it through this after all.

'The information carried by Charlotte is of a sensitive nature. In the hands of the wrong person, it could pose a serious risk to my company. I do apologise for all the theatrics of our little meeting but I had to be certain that you didn't steal the device for the purpose of selling my secrets to the highest bidder.'

I folded my handkerchief and put it back in my pocket.

'That's rich. I don't ever remember going to the theatre and getting my ribs broken. At least you believe me so that's something I guess.'

'Make no mistakes, I don't believe you... not completely,' she replied with a smile, bordering on the sinister. 'But I have no evidence to prove otherwise. So I think it best we part ways for now.'

The Baker entered the dome proper and pulled over at first opportunity. No need to keep me in the car any longer than was necessary. My usefulness had run its course.

'It's the other assailant,' I said as I climbed out.

'I'm sorry?' she replied as she leaned forward to address me.

'The other guy. The one that clocked me. He's the one with the goods now, or at least that's my theory. He's the one that you should be driving around in your car beating the crap out of until he tells you what you want to know.' I left out the part of him looking like Nolan Kitterman because she probably already knew that as well.

'Of course, Mr Helmqvist. I shall look into the matter more fully. Good day to you,' she said as bodyguard No. 1 closed the door and the limo sped off.

Watching them go, I thanked my lucky stars to still be in one piece. Once they'd left my field of vision, I hailed the first available LTI and rode in peace to the nearest health clinic.

X-rays confirmed that I had two fractured ribs. The doc gave me this girdle-thing to help align the ribs, a prescription for some more painkillers and a lollipop for my troubles. I didn't really care too much about the girdle, but the pills would definitely help me through another pain-filled episode of my life.

I hopped into another taxi to Theo's shop in order to retrieve my gym bag from the trunk. En route, we swung by a drug store and I choked down a handful of pills in one gulp. On the ride back to my place, I gave Erica a quick call to see if she wanted to stop by my place when she finished her shift. We agreed on 8pm.

All told, it was around seven when I finally walked through my front door. I made myself a double whisky, neat. Only after the sour mash mingled in my gullet for a few minutes did I dare to have a look in the bathroom mirror. I had bruises in too many places to care about or enumerate. Suffice it to say, I looked like Rocky at the, well, at the end of most of those pictures.

I went back to the living room, drained my glass and had set myself up with another one when an image on my MAX smartwatch showed Erica's gorgeous face looking into a tiny camera.

22

I buzzed Erica in from my MAX and waited for her by the door to my apartment. The smell of delicious greasy food preceded her entrance. Sure enough, she greeted me with a hello and a takeaway carton.

'I thought you might be hungry,' she said as she handed me the container. I peeked in. A Reuben. It looked messy and heavenly.

'Bless you, Erica. I am starving.'

She slipped past me. 'Good. You eat and I'll shower if that's okay with you. I reek of the diner.'

'Help yourself. Towels are in a closet next to the bathroom.'

While Erica showered, I demolished the sandwich and washed it down with a pale ale I found in the fridge. I had just finished when she stepped out of the bathroom clothed in nothing but a towel. Her thick mane of straight, black hair up in a ponytail. Her toned, light brown legs glistening with oil. Transfixed, I watched her head towards the bedroom.

'I thought I'd go in here.' The towel hit the floor when she passed through the doorway. She pulled her hair out of its ponytail and it cascaded down her shoulders. I completely forgot about what few crumbs remained of the sandwich, the beer, the shitty day, everything.

Erica sat on her knees on the bed as I struggled out of my clothes. She guided me down to the mattress. We took it nice and easy. She knew I'd taken a beating today. We hadn't discussed it in any amount of detail, but my body showed all the marks. As before, she took command and we made love with her on top. Gentle. Soft, rhythmic motions. Tender yet powerful. The two of us lost in a moment.

When we finished, she laid down next to me. Her right leg

draped over my left. Her right hand caressing my chest. Minutes passed with nothing but the sound of our breathing.

'Was that too rough on you?' she asked.

'No. No. It was fine.' I turned my head and kissed the top of hers. 'Better than fine, actually.'

'So what happened to you, Danny? You're covered in bruises.'

'Wrong place at the wrong time. Twice, if you can believe it.'

She looked up at me. 'Not really. But I guess you won't go into too much detail.'

It wasn't a question, but I answered it. 'I can't. I'm sorry, Erica. It's related to this case I've been working on.'

'The same case as the one I was questioned on?'

I resisted the urge to apologise again. 'That's the one. Did you want to talk about what happened at the police station?'

Her eyes drifted back down to my chest. 'Not really. There isn't too much to tell. The detective asked where I was Saturday night. I told him the truth. He asked if I was with you the entire night. I told him a lie and stuck to it. I figured if they had something on you, it would come out pretty quick but it never did.'

'I admire your confidence and your smarts. Not many people could pull that off.'

She smiled. 'Lucky for you, I'm not most people.'

We kissed and fooled around until I was ready to go again. We made love the same as before; however, with more intensity. Neither one of us cared about my bruises, cracked ribs or banged-up knee. We rode a wave of passion and endorphins.

The next morning, we stood outside Erica's apartment building once again. I spun my trilby around my right hand on the inner headband.

'We should do this again, Danny. Soon.'

I glanced up at her building and then back into those almond pools of hers. 'I'd like that.'

'Call me later then?'

Unexpectedly, an image of Kitterman and those goons flashed

through my thoughts. What they might do to Erica, if Mara felt she needed leverage against me.

'Let me finish this case up, first. I promised my client two weeks and I intend to give them two weeks.' I stopped spinning my hat and twirled a few locks of her hair into my fingers instead. 'And you are far too distracting for me to give them an earnest two weeks.'

Erica grinned. 'I'll take that as a compliment. But I dunno, Danny.' She took my hat from me and looked down at it briefly. 'First you injure your knee. Then get used as a punching bag—'

'Hey!' I interjected. 'I dished out a little, too.'

'I'm sure you did. All I'm saying is that at this rate, there may not be much left of you by the end of two weeks.'

She was having fun with me now.

'I'll do my best to be in one piece at the end of this.'

'Promise?'

'Promise.'

Erica set my hat atop my head at an angle that I wouldn't normally wear it. I imagined it made me look a bit like Blaine at the end of *Casablanca* but I have no idea.

'Good. Because I like you, Danny, and we're just getting started.' With that, she planted a kiss on my cheek and pushed through the door to her building.

23

The beep of a garbage truck backing down the alley behind my building echoed dimly in my mind as I sat at my desk plotting my next move. The business at the Verne Bottling Company had brought my investigation to a complete standstill. Prudence dictated that I should leave it alone. I no longer had a client, and therefore no longer had a case. Sure, I had told Erica something completely contradictory a few hours earlier, but I didn't think she'd understand my need to chase a theory about the storage device and a ghost who had snatched it out of my grasp.

Pam's voice brought me back into the office.

'You have a visitor, sir.'

'Who?'

'Mara Kitterman.'

I rubbed my eyes and patted my cheek to shake the cobwebs loose. 'Alright.'

In she walked and I struggled to stand.

'Don't bother,' she said as she took a seat. Relief washed over me when her goons didn't appear behind her. She must've left them in the car.

I settled back into my chair. 'What a pleasant surprise. I was just thinking about you, Ms Kitterman.'

She gave the room an appraising once over. She didn't look too impressed. 'You have an outdated android assistant and a shabby office. Life as a PI must be disappointing, Mr Helmqvist.'

'I like what I do well enough and I wouldn't trade Pam in for a dozen 'bots straight off the assembly line. Anyway, I doubt you came all this way to give me career advice.'

'Indeed not. I am here to pay you a reward for finding my android yesterday.'

'Which one? I seem to recall finding two.' A pretty good shot, I thought, and her reaction confirmed it.

'I had also intended to apologise for the way that you were treated yesterday,' she said with eyes narrowed after a few seconds. 'However, I am starting to think that your behaviour does not warrant one.'

My chair groaned loudly on ageing springs as I rocked back in it. 'I'm glad you didn't bring those two meatheads with you today. I'm not sure I like the way they play.'

'Must you make everything so difficult? I am trying to extend an olive branch and you continue to insult me with your glibness.'

I leaned forward, elbows landing on the desk.

'Your type annoys the hell out of me. You think that you can buy off anyone who gets in your way and make them forget about everything else that doesn't concern you, and you alone. I don't want your money or your goddamn branch.'

She sat there for a moment, seething. I doubt anyone spoke to her with my level of candour. Rich, successful, brilliant people like her usually get what they want. They also find themselves surrounded by a chorus of yes-men and women who sing their praises and bolster an illusion of infallibility.

'Very well, Mr Helmqvist,' she said with strained civility as she stood up. 'If that is how you feel, then I shall bid you good day.'

On her way out, she looked back one last time. 'I wish you success in all of your future endeavours.'

'Yeah. Sure. See you around, Ms Kitterman.'

As soon as I heard the outer door close, I returned to my position of staring out the window and stewing in my own thoughts. The creak of tired upholstery alerted me to the presence of another in the room. I spun around to find Pam sitting in the same seat Kitterman had vacated.

'Sir? If I may ask, what was that about?'

'Kitterman offered to pay me a reward for finding her androids.'

'Androids, sir?'

'Well, she said it was money for finding Rennick's body but I do not doubt the other one, James, has a MARA Corporation stamp on him somewhere.'

'Did you accept the money?'

'No. I didn't. She may have called it a reward, but it was a bribe... another fishing expedition. Maybe she thought some credits would buy her the truth about what I know. I will say she's far more intuitive than I would've guessed.'

'I am worried about your safety.'

'Worried? What?' On cue, I winced from a jolt of pain.

'If your summations have been accurate, sir, threat of death is the next logical step. Mara Kitterman has tried to intimidate you, followed by an offer of monetary compensation. In both instances, you have frustrated her attempt by your refusal. If she suspects you know something about her past, putting you down for a dirt nap would ensure your silence.'

'A dirt nap?' I tried to laugh but gave up.

'Did I use the colloquialism incorrectly?' Her concern seemed genuine.

'No. I just didn't expect to hear it coming outta your mouth.'

'It seemed appropriate within the context.'

The gravity of her worry for my safety didn't sit well and I shifted in my seat. Pam was right. Kitterman might resort to more drastic means. By all accounts, the murder of one person would barely register on her moral radar. The bitch had killed thousands.

'I appreciate you telling me this, Pam, but I doubt she'd risk anything so drastic. She probably already knows I don't have anything on her or the police would be involved. Not to mention the late-comer to the old Verne plant could have left me on the ground in a state far worse than unconscious.'

'Agreed. I am merely expressing my position on the current situation.'

'It means a lot to me, Pam. It does... even if it's a tad strange.'

She tilted her head down in a quick nod, stood, and returned to her desk without another word. The only change to this routine: she did not start banging on her keyboard with determination. She just stared at it.

Left alone in my office again, I couldn't shake off what Pam had said. I felt broken and vulnerable. I wanted nothing more than the feel of a gun against my damaged ribs and the company of faces I trusted. To that end, I made two phone calls. The first to Theo, telling him I was on my way. The second to Steve, for a ride across the district. He told me he'd be outside in 10.

'I'm done for the day. If anyone calls, take a message. I'll call you later to check in,' I told Pam as I hobbled by her desk.

She watched me leave through quiet, expressionless eyes. Any amount of concern she did have for my safety was hidden deep inside her electronic circuitry. The *tap-tap-tap* of her keyboard filled the silence as I stepped into the hallway.

'Where to?' Steve asked as I eased myself into the cab.

'Theo's Hi-Tech Automotive.'

He punched the name into his nav unit. 'Over on Harper?'

'That's the one.'

'It's not very far from here,' he mused out loud.

'I know. I'm just not feelin' too great at the moment.'

He glanced up in the review mirror at me once again. 'If you don't mind me saying, Mr Helmqvist, you don't look too good. Are you sure you wouldn't rather go see a doctor or something?'

I winced out a chuckle.

'Thanks, Steve. I've already been to the doc's. Right now, I need to see a man about a car.'

'A car? I didn't know you drive.'

Not an uncommon reaction. A lot of people go their entire life-time without getting a licence.

'I do. And I have a pretty sweet ride.'

'What happened to it, if you don't mind me askin'?'

'Nothing too serious. One of the doors won't shut properly.'

'Is it because your head was in the way?' Steve asked as he merged into traffic.

'Real funny,' I said before we got too far. 'Listen, I'd like to make a pit stop on the way to the shop.'

'Sure thing. You're paying the fare. We can go wherever you want.'

'There's a barbecue joint nearby. Theo loves their food.'

At Tunnel BBQ, I ordered two Memphis Platters with an extra order of fried potato wedges. One was for me and the other was for my mechanic. I figured he'd appreciate the gesture and I needed him to agree to a favour.

Steve looked around cautiously as we pulled into Theo's. 'This is where you brought your car?'

'Don't let the ambience fool you, Steve. Theo is as good as they come. In fact, I doubt you'll find a better mechanic in all of New London.'

'You'd never guess.'

I placed my thumb against the chip reader and paid the fare. Tip included. 'Appearances and deception and all that.'

He chuckled. 'True. Need any help getting out?'

'I think I can manage,' and I grimaced and groaned my way out of the back seat, contents within the carry-out bag undamaged.

Steve poked his head out his window. 'Call me if you need anything, Mr Helmqvist. You're turning out to be a very profitable friend to have.'

Friend. I have no idea if he meant it, but when he said it my spirits rose higher than they'd been in days.

I nodded and waved. 'Warms my heart to hear you say that Steve.' Sarcasm appreciated. He drove off with his left hand sticking out the window in goodbye.

Theo was parked behind a service computer watching a video of a dog chasing a stick in low gravity. His eyes crinkled in delight. His laughter rolled out like a Christmas carol.

'Daniel,' he said with his mellow baritone voice. 'To what do I owe the pleasure?' His gaze drifted down to the Tunnel BBQ logo on the side of the plastic bag.

'I've brought you a bribe.' I hoisted the dinner up onto the counter.

'A bribe?' he responded with mock offence. 'I am an honest man, Daniel. You know that.'

'To a fault,' I countered. 'But I had hoped you'd loan me one of your jalopies while the Griffon is being repaired. I figured some barbecue would help my case.'

He pulled one of the containers out.

'If it wasn't for the fact that you brought me this delicious-smelling meal, I'd be hurt at the thought of any of my very fine automobiles being referred to as a *jalopy*.'

'Is that a yes, then?' I said with a chuckle.

'Of course you can borrow one of my cars, Daniel. However,' he continued after a brief pause, 'it isn't going to take that long to fix the Nash. Most of the damage was superficial.'

'Ah, I see. Could you take a bit longer to fix it? Like a week or so? And while we are on the subject of my car, I would like to retrieve the items I left in the trunk.'

'No problem, my friend.' There it was again. Friend. It felt good. 'Now, what about this car you want to borrow?'

'Something for a little surveillance work. I thought maybe you'd have something that might blend in a bit better than my car.'

Theo stood there and contemplated my request.

'I think I have just the thing. Come with me.'

We walked out of the customer service area, through the garage with its four work bays, and out a door in the back. I was greeted with a whole host of cars in various states of repair (or disrepair might be a more accurate descriptor).

'Here we go,' Theo said after a few minutes of scanning the yard and led me over to a faded black LTI.

'This?' I said, as I gave it the once over. As far as I could tell, it used to be a taxi but one that had seen better days. Theo laughed a hearty laugh. One of those laughs that comes booming straight from your toes.

'It runs fine. It just needs a good wash. But it is perfect. You can pretend to be a cab driver. No one will suspect a thing.'

I scratched my chin and thought about it. I doubt anyone would even notice me in RD1. There are hundreds of taxis at all times milling about the place. Its shabby appearance might discourage any potential fares.

'You do have a point. I'll take it.'

He patted my shoulder and I winced. He didn't seem to notice.

'I'll have my boys get it cleaned up. While we wait, let's see what's in those containers.' My stomach rumbled in agreement.

On the way to his office, we swung by the Griffon. Theo's boys had the door off and one of them had finished cutting off the mangled hinge. I fired up the electronics, disabled the secret compartment's lock, and the boss man himself snagged my satchel full of contraband.

We were elbow deep in sauce-stained napkins and bones when a shop guy popped in to tell us the LTI was good to go.

'Don't you go messing up the doors on this taxi, Daniel. You hear me?' He laughed at his own joke and the sound filled the room.

'No promises but I'll do my best.'

Theo slapped me on the back again, still laughing. I took the blow as best I could. He handed me the keys. We shook hands. And he stood leaning against the perimeter fence of his little empire, watching me drive into the sunset.

In the amount of time it took me to walk from the parking structure to my building, reason gave way to fear. An alley loomed like a potential ambush spot. Imaginary thugs crept in the shadows. By the time I reached my apartment, sweat glistened on my forehead, and I waited for the bogeyman to come.

Nothing happened over night. No unseen assassins burst through my door and murdered me in my sleep. No mysterious intruders skulked their way into my apartment and went through my personal effects while I dreamt the night away.

I woke to a day that began, like so many others, rather unremarkably and for that I was grateful. Being fortunate enough to catch the sun rise over Mars, and any amount of relief associated with that feeling, didn't stop me from scrolling through my list of contacts and hitting a familiar number.

'Detective John Ashdown, Metro Police,' he said automatically.

'John. It's Daniel Helmqvist.'

'You alright, Helm? You sound a little out of sorts.'

'You're gonna think I'm suffering from post-concussion delusions, but…' I held my breath for two Mississippis before continuing. 'But if you find my corpse stuffed in a trash bin or missing over the next few days or weeks, don't say I didn't warn you.'

'What the hell! What are you mixed up in now?'

'I won't go into specifics, but let's just say hospitality in this city ain't what it used to be.'

'Someone roughed you up, again?'

'That's one way to put it.'

'Did you report the incident?'

'No, but I did go to the doctors.'

'Good for you. And you think it's connected to a case you're working on?'

'Not really. I dunno for certain, but my office assistant does, though. I think she's worried about me.'

'What's your assistant's name?'

'Pam.'

'Surname?'

'No last name. She's an android.'

'Wait! You have a bucket of bolts that believes your life may be in danger and it's worried about you? How is that even possible?'

'Beats the hell outta me. Crazy, isn't it?'

'That's one way to put it. And you believe her?'

'Her argument has a certain logic that is difficult to refute.'

Silence on the other end. 'You were right. I do think you've been knocked on the head too hard. But even if your assistant is correct, what do you want me to do about it?'

'Nothing, John. But it's like I said before: if your department is called to a crime scene and my dead ass is in the middle of it, don't rule it accidental or suicide.'

'Christ, Helm, if this is some attempt at a joke, your gallows humour isn't appreciated.'

'No joke, Detective. A heads-up is all.'

'Well, I can guarantee you one thing.'

'What's that?'

'No one'll try to ice you while you're in my interrogation room.'

'How very comforting.'

'Well, while we're on the subject—'

'Which you brought up.'

'I'd like to speak to you again about the embezzlement case.'

'We can't do this over the phone?'

'I'd rather talk in person. If it helps, I'll have a hot cup of coffee waiting for you.'

'I guess I better hurry then. The lukewarm sludge you fed me last time was on the wrong side of awful.'

'Yeah, better hurry.' And with that he hung up on me.

24

Ashdown stepped through the door into the interrogation room with a steaming cup of Joe in one hand and the requisite MIX in the other. The scent of Arabica beans filled the tiny space.

The detective took the seat across from me and launched right into it. 'Sorry to keep you waiting but I figured I'd hold off on the coffee until I had proof of life.'

'Ha ha ha. Maybe you can tell me why I'm here instead of the comedy routine.' I tested the java and scalded the tip of my tongue. Ashdown caught my recoil from the sip and grinned.

He then pulled something up on his tablet and passed it over to me.

'What's this?'

'Just read.'

I stared at an MNN article about an industrial accident that had happened a few hours ago. I skimmed the page until I saw what Ashdown wanted me to see.

A spokesperson, for Revolve Systems Ltd, released the names of the three individuals: Sarah Oliver, Luther Dwerry and Henrietta Perez.

'What the hell?' I said without looking up. 'Shouldn't Dwerry be in lock-up and not getting skewered by a robotic welder?'

'Porter didn't press charges. We released all three of them on Friday.'

I looked up now. 'All of them? Even his assistant?'

'Yep. Free on Friday. Dead two days later.'

'Wait, you're telling me they are all dead?'

Ashdown took the MIX back from me. 'Sorry. Only Dwerry – that we know of.'

'What's that supposed to mean?' I tested the coffee again; drinkable in very small quantities.

'Keep in mind this is all happening in real time, but we only have the known whereabouts of two out of the three in the embezzlement case.'

'I'm assuming Dwerry, who is now in the morgue. And?'

'Lyric Voss. Cooper is in the wind. We have him going into his apartment on Friday and then nothing. We sent a unit over to investigate and there's no sign of him. No sign of a struggle. No sign he took any of his possessions.'

'Cooper is in the wind? How could he be in the wind? We live in domes. It isn't like he could sneak away in the cover of night, never to be seen again.'

'If he is still in New London, we'll find him. Like I said, this only started to matter when we got a report of Dwerry's death.'

'Do you think Porter is involved?'

'That's the question of the day, Helm.'

'Is HTS connected to Revolve in any way?'

'Revolve make propulsion components for DRIVE, who build FTL systems. It all uses superconductors, and HTS is listed as a supplier to Revolve. HTS has purchased engines from DRIVE in the past, but so has just about every other corporation and government with enough credits to afford their high-end Space Fold technology. But that's about as far as the connection goes. Nothing obvious. However, it doesn't mean he couldn't have orchestrated it somehow.'

I nursed my coffee and reflected on what Ashdown had told me. If Porter was behind this, he was playing a dangerous game.

'I don't understand. Why did Porter drop the charges?'

A question I could answer. He didn't trust how the investigation would play out – he wanted to control the situation as much as possible – but I wanted Ashdown's version.

'He said that the recovery of the money was more important than ruining the lives of such talented young people.'

I nearly spat my coffee out. 'What the hell? He said that??'

Ashdown nodded. 'I think he referred to Ms Voss more than the other two. Still, it sounds like a ton of horse shit to me.'

'Earlier, you said you knew the whereabouts of two of the three. The second being Voss, right?'

'Yep, I contacted her at her known address.'

'You actually spoke to her?'

'We did. I asked her if she knew about what had happened to Dwerry. She hadn't heard anything about him. I also asked her why she thought Porter didn't press charges for her role in the embezzlement case. She confirmed what Porter had already told us. She said he told her that she had great potential but had fallen in with the wrong crowd.'

Porter's butler accent floated through my mind. 'I hate to say it, but it does sound like something he would say. The guy stepped right out of period drama and into our century.'

Ashdown continued. 'Voss told me that not only did she not get sacked for her involvement in the plot but that Porter was transferring her to their Lares office. She called it a promotion of sorts.'

'Do you believe her?'

The detective tapped his chin in thought. 'I dunno. Her voice carried a nervous energy and she seemed distracted during our interview. However, a simultaneous chat with Porter at his home by another detective supported her story. He said he thought she would do well outside the influence of a bad egg like Cooper. Voss confirmed it independently.'

I ran the heel of my palm and my fingers back and forth over my forehead, trying to make sense of this. For the moment, I'd forgotten all about my involvement in this little caper.

'So let me get this straight – Voss plays a critical role in the theft of three million credits from HTS and not only is she not facing prison but she's getting a promotion?'

'Looks that way, Helm.'

'Where is Lares?'

Ashdown jabbed at the MIX's touchscreen. 'Gliese 667 C system.'

'And HTS has an office there.'

More jabbing. 'Umm, yeah. They have a partnership with a local government on a solar farm project.'

We sat there for a moment, looking at each other. I still had no idea why the detective had called me in.

'He said "bad egg"?' I asked finally.

'What's that?'

'You said Porter called Cooper a "bad egg".'

'Oh, right. Yeah. A bad egg.'

'From anyone other than him, I'd be surprised to hear that dusty old phrase.'

'What can you tell me about Porter?'

Ah ha! Now his calling me in started to make sense. Information.

'I doubt I can tell you more than you already now. CEO of HTS for some time now. Immigrated to Mars with the job. He has some high-level political connections within the city. Plays golf with the DA at one of those ridiculous virtual country clubs. A weakness for misguided employees apparently.' I shrugged. 'That's about it. The guy hired me to do a job and I did it.'

'That's it?'

'Afraid so.'

Ashdown shut off the MIX and stood. I took it as my cue and stood as well.

'Thanks for coming in Dan.' We headed to the door of the interview room.

I stepped through first. 'No problem. Sorry I couldn't be more help.'

Ashdown and I headed to the elevators.

'Do you think he did it?' I asked as I entered the first available carriage and held the door open.

He stepped in beside me.

'Hard to say. The investigation is young but nothing directly connects Porter to the accident. I doubt we will find anything. One more question before we part ways.'

'Fire away.'

He jammed the Emergency Stop button. A computerised voice filled the space.

> The Emergency Stop button has been activated. If this is an actual emergency, please say 'Emergency' in a clear, audible voice and someone will be with your shortly. Thank you and have a nice day.

'Why did Porter hire you for an embezzlement case? Why not keep it in-house? Use his own people?'

I shrugged again. 'Beats me, Ash. Maybe he didn't know who to trust within the organisation. Everything pointed to an inside job when he came to me with it. He went outside HTS to a person he trusted, who in turn recommended me. I took the case and, because of it, get to keep the lights on for a little while longer.'

Ashdown pressed the Ground Floor button again and the elevator resumed its slow descent.

'Fair enough,' he said as the doors opened.

I hopped out. He didn't.

'Stay out of trouble, Helm.'

'Always do, Detective.'

Given my slight paranoia of being killed, or abducted, or abducted and then killed, using public transportation may not have been considered smart, but the proliferation of commuters and security cameras made an untimely death improbable at the very least.

I jumped off near Tireman, swung by my office. From my perch on the corner of Pam's desk, I updated her on my day.

'Do you believe Mr Porter killed Luther Dwerry?' she asked when I had finished.

'I honestly don't know. The obvious answer is yes. However, I can't imagine why he'd risk it. He'd have to know he'd be a suspect given the fact that Dwerry had just been arrested for stealing from him.'

'If he did have Mr Dwerry killed, do you think Detective Ashdown will find evidence that leads to Porter's involvement?'

I dropped my trilby on my knee. 'He didn't seem too sure when I left but the accident only just happened. Something might turn up, but I'd be surprised.'

'Perhaps his ego forced him into a reckless action.'

'I don't see it, Pam. Porter is definitely an arrogant bastard but killing Dwerry days after he'd been released is *too* careless.'

'Thus far it has achieved a desirable end.'

'Explain.'

'Ms Voss is leaving Mars of her own volition—'

'I'm certain this isn't because of her own volition,' I cut in. Pam glared. She hated being interrupted.

'Of her *professed* own volition, then. Alvin Cooper cannot be found. And, Luther Dwerry's death served two purposes. One, he no longer poses a threat to Mr Porter. Two, the fear that they might be next has probably contributed to Ms Voss's willingness to leave the planet and Mr Cooper's disappearance.'

'Cooper might be dead in a cave somewhere outside the domes for all we know.'

'Unlikely. Discovery of the body would throw even more suspicion on Porter.'

'True.'

'My guess is that he used his IT talents to sneak out of his apartment and secure passage off Mars. Possibly to Earth, where he could vanish into the teeming mass of humanity who call that planet "home".' She said that last part with a tinge of revulsion. Such a strange robot.

'Well it doesn't really matter now. It's out of our hands.'

Pam started to respond but checked herself.

'What?'

'Nothing, sir.' To ensure I didn't persist, she started typing the notes of our conversation on her keyboard at a furious pace.

'Easy or I'll have to replace that keyboard by the day's end.'

She didn't stop.

I hopped off her desk and made for the entrance.

'Where are you going?' she asked over the sound of rattling keys.

I held the door open but looked back at my assistant, who did not look at me.

'To pick up a car and watch MARA Corporation. Maybe something will happen with that case. Maybe not, but it's the only play I have at the moment.'

'Be careful.'

'It's just sitting in a car.'

Her expression darkened a split second and the chatter from her keyboard stopped.

'My concern for your safety still holds. Probability dictates that she will try to kill you at some point.'

'Gee, thanks.' Unease crept up my spine. 'You have such a way with words.'

'Just be careful, sir.'

'I'll do my best. If it helps, I'll check in at the end of the day.'

I caught the door before it closed and poked my head back into the office. 'I nearly forgot! Arrange a meeting with Porter for Wednesday. Tell him we need to talk and that he should have my credits ready.'

She replied with a 'yes, sir' and more typing.

As I drove Theo's LTI from the CD to RD1, Pam's parting comments hung in the air and led to uncomfortable questions.

Would Kitterman try to kill me?

A fleeting image of Nolan Kitterman and two visits from Mara in as many days had to do. He could have done the job but didn't. However, I had no idea what his purpose was in this story.

And the concerned look on Pam's face a few minutes ago. What was that all about?

The unsettling realisation that I was the only loose end in the HTS case hit me. Dwerry was dead. Accident or otherwise. Voss had been turned. Cooper had vanished. That left me. Pam wanted to say something to this effect but didn't. Another question.

New London began to feel very small. I gripped the wheel and hit the accelerator.

The rearview and side cameras revealed nothing but my anxiety. Still, it felt good to zip through town. The cab handled like a brand new car and the seats had enough padding to make sitting on my ass for stretches at a time not too unpleasant a prospect. By the time I hit the heart of downtown, my nerves settled down. I needed to be smart, not scared. If I could do that, I'd be okay.

After cruising around RD1 and the four streets framing MARA Corporation for a couple of hours, I started to get a sense for the rhythms of the district. I soon found a few places where I could stop with a good view of the main entrance.

Tiny cameras installed on the roof by the 'New London Taxi' sign, plus the cameras that came as standard equipment, gave me nearly 360 coverage from inside the car. The video feeds filled small boxes on the left and right side of my MIX12 screen. I sat parked kerbside with baseball highlights taking up the centre of the area of my tablet, ignoring the world outside as much as possible. The duffle bag with my super-suit lay on the front passenger floorboard. I kept the NEEDLE in a shoulder holster, hidden by the same jacket I wore to Cooper's place. In fact, as I took a quick glance in the mirror, my 'taxi driver' disguise looked a lot like my 'pizza delivery guy' disguise.

I hung around, fending off potential fares and trying to keep my movements as random as possible. About 10 minutes past 11pm, an all too familiar Baker Electric rolled through MARA Corp's security checkpoint and hung a left. I followed until I knew it was heading towards Res 1. A return to her robot empire confirmed little to no activity.

Between Monday and Wednesday, I'd gotten pretty good at sitting in a car and moving around just enough to keep New Londoners out of my taxi. The benefit of a few days of inactivity was that I started to heal. Bruises became less tender and I could breathe easier with each passing day.

Somewhere in all of that, Porter and I agreed to meet at HTS on Wednesday afternoon. At 4.30am, I left RD1 through the north tunnel connecting it to Research District 2 and prayed for nothing to happen at MARA Corp in my absence.

When I arrived at HTS, I told the tasty dish behind the counter I had an appointment with Porter. A few minutes later he stepped out the elevator and motioned for me to follow him. Like an obedient child, I did as instructed.

He stopped in front of a glass display with a model of a mag-lev train racing around a round track with a map of Europe in the centre. I sidled up beside Porter and watched as the train made circuit after circuit. Going nowhere. Every minute of every day.

'Did you know that this model is a replica of our very first project, Mr Helmqvist?' he asked, also staring at it.

I could see the reflection in the glass of me shaking my head. 'I didn't.' I didn't really care, either, but I let it stand at that.

'A high-speed rail system from London to Rome and all points Continental. The network spread like a spider's web and our super-conductors made fast, safe travel to virtually any major city in Europe possible. From there, HTS expanded to become the galactic success that it is today.'

The motion of the train was hypnotic. 'HTS got its hands pretty dirty along the way.'

'Humph. All organisations of importance have skeletons in their closet. It's the price of doing business. The key is to ensure that either no one opens the door to that closet, or they cannot even find it in the first place. My complacency nearly cost us a great deal. A mistake I will not make in the future.'

'Is that why you didn't press charges on Voss, Cooper and Dwerry? To ensure your secrets remained secret? To control the situation as much as possible?'

'I couldn't be certain your tactics would survive an investigation, Mr Helmqvist. No offence to your ability, but I could not risk it. I do believe I was quite clear in the beginning that this was never about the money. It was about controlling information. Any quibbling I may have done about money was merely posturing. Others need to believe it is about money and nothing else.'

'I know your secret too. Does that make me a liability? Am I due for an accident?'

His laugh seemed forced to me and he turned his head to look at me for the first time. 'Don't be preposterous, you came highly recommended to me by a friend. In fact, you are one of the few people I trust with this secret.'

I noticed he neither confirmed nor denied any involvement in Dwerry's death, but I let that slide too. 'I'll remember to pass my gratitude along to Han the next time I see him.' The DA and I had fallen out of contact soon after I left his office. It's why his vouching for me seemed so strange.

Porter turned to face me. I followed suit. 'Right. Well, you held up your end of the bargain. I believe all that is left to conclude our business is your fee. If you could provide me with a routing number, I can deposit the funds into your account at this very moment.'

He produced a mini MIX5 from his breast pocket, and I provided a routing number to my business account. He pecked away on the touchscreen with a stylus. 'Done and done,' he announced after a few seconds.

I pulled up my account on my MAX smartwatch. The balance increased by 30 grand. 'You've overpaid,' I said as I looked from the watch to him.

'Nonsense, Mr Helmqvist. You have done HTS and myself a great service. Consider it a bonus based on performance.'

In other words, a bribe. Unlike Kitterman's earlier, I decided I didn't mind taking this one.

Porter extended his hand. I hesitated a second before shaking it.

'Good day to you, Mr Helmqvist.'

'Yeah. See you around, Porter.'

Walking back down the carpet and through the set of glass double doors felt like an escape. Like I had just cheated death.

25

With the HTS case closed, the growing sense of dread began to lessen. With that passage of time, the pain in my ribs began to subside, as well. It allowed me to log a few hours of FE9 training before I turned in for the night. The LTI worked fine for surveillance but the rooftops would be better. I could actually see over the wall and risk a peek through the skylight of the R&D building. In my week on the ground, I could see light streaming out of it every night until 11pm. Roughly 15 minutes later, Kitterman's limo would pull out onto Corporation North.

The alley behind my apartment made the perfect spot to practise. Jumps, drops, thrusts, honing my balance for the use of the lev units in the boots. I worked at it until fatigue made me reckless. By the end of that week, I had a better understanding of how the suit functioned. I wouldn't say I was ready to take my act pro or anything. But, at least I felt like I could avoid any more disasters like that first night.

After that, I split my time. During daylight hours, I prowled the area in my cab. However, when the sun went down, I made a quick change and took to the world above the streets. Despite my comfort level rising in the FE9, the first jump from one building to the next sent the butterflies in my gut into a tizzy. My confidence increased, however, with each jump, landing and slide.

All the while, I pushed aside thoughts about what the hell I had hoped to accomplish. I had no reason to believe the storage device still existed or that Nolan Kitterman was anything more than a figment of my imagination. But I had no other course of action. So I persisted.

A couple of days into my new routine, I decided to get a look through Mara's skylight. I could have made the jump from several places but went from the same alley I did over a week ago. I have no idea why I picked it. Perhaps to compare how far I'd come along.

Tucked behind the corner of a building, I bolted across the street, arced over the wall with a quick burst from the jetpack, touched down for a split second and launched myself upwards. I landed with all the grace of a sparrow on a telephone wire.

The success of my jump filled me with all kinds of misplaced optimism. My heart raced with excitement and I stole over to the rooftop window. I expected to find Mara and Nolan huddled over a table, the video plans of the UN attack streaming on a holo-display. Father and daughter teetering with maniacal glee. Instead, what I got was a glimpse of Mara leaving a large, open workshop and the lights going out. An infrared scan revealed nothing.

If I had given up at that very moment, I'd like to think I wouldn't be judged too harshly. That no one would call me a quitter. Fortunately, I returned the next night and was rewarded for my efforts.

When I peered down through the skylight, a butt naked, and very much alive – for lack of a better term – Charlotte Rennick stood in front of Kitterman. By her precise movements and head gestures that followed Kitterman's hands, she must have been going through some diagnostic tests. Seeing her filled me with renewed optimism. Whether or not she remembered me, I hadn't lost a client. A silly notion perhaps. But in many ways, it validated these last few days.

Two days later, vigilance rewarded me in a big way.

Mara Kitterman worked alone on something I couldn't make out because her body blocked it from view. Suddenly, she looked up and over to a specific place. Someone had entered the lab.

A moment later, Nolan Kitterman stepped into view. He wore a familiar-looking bomber jacket and flat cap. I gripped the edge of the skylight. My heart pounded as adrenaline coursed through my every muscle. The moment had come.

I circled the skylight to try to grab a couple of screen shots with my visor. His hat prevented me from getting portrait perfect images. However, they were better than nothing – so long as you accepted the fact that the person in the images had returned from the grave.

Jumping through the skylight, interrupting their scene and

yelling 'gotcha' didn't strike me as a very good plan. In all likelihood, Papa Kitterman would kick my ass again and Mara would have me dead to rights.

Fortunately, Nolan made the choice for me. He gave Mara a warm, paternal hug. She handed him a device that looked very similar to the one that I had lifted from her office. He stuffed it into his jacket pocket, and grabbed a satchel from off the workspace. They exchanged goodbyes, and he disappeared stage right. I ran in the same direction to the edge of the roof and waited. Sure enough, Nolan Kitterman stepped out into the night and headed for a service entrance door in the east wall of the complex.

Once through, he turned right and made his way towards Franklin. When he had gone far enough, I made a double jump to clear the wall. Another quick boost sent me up onto a nearby building.

'Call Pam,' I whispered into headgear.

She picked up on the third ring. 'Good evening, sir.'

'Pam! I have eyes on Nolan Kitterman. He's in RD1 on Franklin. Can you access the street cameras and follow him?'

'One second to power up my computer. Okay, I have him on my screen now. Black coat and cap. That is him, correct?'

'Yeah, that's Kitterman. Tell me where he's going. I need to stop by my car and lose some of this gear.'

'Very well, sir. I shall notify you of his every move.'

I retraced my steps to my taxi and dropped down into a nearby alley. I tucked the gloves and helmet into the FE9's backpack and ran to my car for a quick back-seat change. I wiggled into my jeans and shirt over the suit. I hopped out, threw my jacket on, pocketed my NEEDLE and locked the backpack in the LTI's trunk. Pam's uninflected voice came over my earwig right as I hit the lock button on the car's fob.

'Kitterman has just entered the Franklin Street Underground station.'

'Gotcha. Thanks, Pam.' I had some ground to cover. I broke

into a sprint. 'How long until the next train?' I called out in laboured breaths.

'Four minutes.'

That should give me enough time.

Caution demanded that I stop and take a quick survey of the street level as I neared the entrance to the station. No sign of Kitterman. I raced down the steps with the urgency of a man late for work.

The stop at Franklin only had one platform. And while that's great and all, if I didn't see which direction he was going to use, I had a 50/50 chance of getting on the wrong train. Pam could probably tell me, but we could only push our luck so far with hacking city cameras before getting caught. If I missed him, or picked the wrong train, then fine. She can help. However, for the moment, doing it the old-fashioned way seemed like the safest option.

I paid at the turnstile and walked hurriedly towards the platform. I peeked around the corner and spotted Kitterman a few metres ahead of me.

If he noticed that anyone was tailing him, he didn't let on. He stood on the platform between the two mag-lev lines like a man without a care in the world. It seemed strange that he didn't try to hide his appearance but then I doubted that anyone would recognise him. People don't expect to see ghosts waiting beside them for the next subway train to arrive. I imagine that to them he looked like a 50-year-old man doing whatever middle-aged people do at this time of night.

I ducked behind one of the pillared arches that helped support the tunnel and separate one direction from the other. When the train arrived, I snuck into the car one down from his. I was close to him but not too close. Thirty seconds later, the train doors shut and we trundled off towards the IM by way of Res 3.

Voice command kept getting 'Call Ashdown' wrong. I had to scroll through my contacts to find his number. He answered on the back end of a yawn.

'Ash. This is Helmqvist.'

CHAPTER TWENTY-FIVE

'Do you know what time it is?'

'Of course I do. Look, I don't have a lot of time. I have Nolan Kitterman in my sights. We are on the F Line from RD1 to the IM. Can you meet me here?'

'I'm sorry. Did you say Nolan Kitterman?'

'Yeah. Nolan Kitterman.'

'He's dead, Helm. Been dead a long time if I recall correctly.'

'Well, I'm telling you he's in the next car over.'

Seconds passed. Ashdown sighed. 'Alright, Helm. Tell me where.'

'I'm not sure exactly. I'll text you when we stop.'

'Fine. Fine. I'm on my way.'

With so few people out, I had to pull my ball cap down low on my forehead and slouch as much as possible. Kitterman stood, which made keeping an eye on him easier but harder to stay out of view. Still, at every stop, I'd peer through the windows in an effort to catch a glimpse of him exiting.

Finally at the Waterman Station in the IM, he did.

I waited until the last possible second before sprinting out and behind a support pillar. And, as improbable as it seemed, Nolan Kitterman continued on at his care-free pace. I fired a message to Ashdown and waited a few minutes before following Kitterman out of the station. On the way up the steps, I patted my right jacket pocket and felt a familiar shape. The NEEDLE hadn't left me under mysterious circumstances.

When I made it out to the surface, there stood Nolan Kitterman in the middle of the deserted street, waiting for me.

26

Nolan and I squared off like a couple of gunslingers in a duel to the death. The only thing missing was the odd piece of tumbleweed blowing past us and Morricone playing in the background.

'You're a very persistent man, Daniel Helmqvist.' A hint of an Oxford accent played at the fringes of his tone. 'However, I fear that our little cat and mouse game has come to an end.'

I had no idea if that was a threat or merely a statement of fact. Either way, I tensed up.

'You're one to talk, Kitterman.'

'What do you mean?'

'You were the one following me at the start of this case, right?'

'Guilty as charged,' he replied with a grin and a nod. 'However, other matters pulled my attentions elsewhere. You can imagine my surprise at the amount of mischief you could get into in such a short amount of time. Your persistence necessitated my return but now I must leave this city.'

'Do you have the storage device that lunatic android ripped outta Charlotte Rennick?' I asked, trying to buy more time for Ashdown to show up. Much to my surprise, he actually answered me.

'Yes,' he said and pulled it from his pocket. 'It's right here.'

'Does it contain information concerning the planning and execution of an attack on the headquarters of the United Nations that took place five years ago?'

'I think that we both know the answer to that question.'

'Then why has she kept it?' I replied and took a few steps towards Nolan, narrowing the gap to about 10 metres. 'It is the one piece of evidence that would ruin her. Everything she has created, her entire life's work, would collapse around her if that information was ever made public.'

'Why do we keep anything? We cling to old, useless things as though they are the keys to our memories. My daughter is a sentimental person, Mr Helmqvist. In this regard, she is no different than anyone else.' His eyes narrowed at my approach. I immediately regretted the decision.

'You mean to tell me the knowledge of countless deaths and the media coverage that followed aren't enough of a reminder? Is the datapad nothing more than a trophy that sociopaths like her enjoy collecting from their victims?'

'Tut tut. There is no need to be cruel. The UN bombing wasn't about media coverage. It was about making a point. A reminder to the world's leaders that they must protect their borders against further harm done to Earth's great epicentres of civilisation by the continual influx of ignorant degenerates. An event to spark serious discussion.'

'Bullshit. Answering the question, "What kind of sick bastard would do this?" is the only discussion this *event* sparked. No one talked about immigration policy in the aftermath. The only thing terrorism ever achieves is senseless death. You're smart enough to know that.' As that last sentence escaped my lips, I prepared to be murdered. He never moved. His feet stayed firmly planted. *Whew!*

'Don't be too certain of that. The American colonists mounted an effective campaign of terror, which led to the formation of a new country. And generally, history bears proof that change – radical, meaningful change – is often precluded by violence.' He paused for a moment. The growing fervour in his eyes subsided.

Where the hell was Ashdown?!

He began again but with more subdued tone. 'Besides, the storage device contains more than just the final wishes of a dying man. There is also the voice and encouragement of a very important person in her life. The one person who ever meant anything to her. The one person who protected her from the cruelties of the world. The one person who guided her through life and gave her a sense of purpose.'

'You.'

'That's right, Mr Helmqvist.' He slipped the device back into his pocket. 'In the end, an interactive holographic programme I had installed on the unit meant too much for her to simply destroy it. It was all that she had left of me.'

'She could have separated the two. For a genius like her, it should be child's play to do so.'

He shrugged. 'As I said, my Mara is a sweet, sentimental person. I have no answer beyond that.'

Keep him talking. Wait for the opportunity.

'Are you Transilience?' As I asked the question, I flexed my right hand and visualised drawing the stun gun. Maybe I could take him unawares.

'My, my... so many questions. Yes, I am. As was the unit who blew up the UN compound. As is James, who you met at that abandoned warehouse.' He paused for dramatic effect. 'As is Ms Rennick. There are, or were, four of us in the Transilience project.'

'I'm guessing the fourth unit was a clone of Paul Fischer, the guy arrested for the actual bombing, and had a built-in explosive device?'

Kitterman nodded. 'Yes, on both accounts.'

'The nature of his construction must have blocked, or fooled, their detectors,' I said out loud; more to myself than Kitterman. He answered anyway.

'Brilliant deduction!'

Man, I hated this guy, but with no sign of Ashdown, I continued my stall tactics.

'Why didn't you take Charlotte to the warehouse instead of that James character?'

'Because I was following you. Ms Rennick was taken to the IM by James to test a theory and to remove the datapad as a precaution. He was the only other person Mara could trust with her secret.'

'What theory?'

'That you had had contact with Charlotte and given her some sort of tracking device. A clever design, I should admit.'

'Gee, thanks.'

Where the hell could Ashdown be??

'James took Ms Rennick to the warehouse to retrieve the storage device and arrange a false crime scene. I trailed you to monitor your actions. When you went straight to the location of James and Charlotte, I waited in the shadows to see how things would play out.'

'You've gotten better Nolan. I'll give you that. I had no idea you were on my tail.'

'Why thank you. Nevertheless, when you disabled James, I was forced to intervene for fear that you might actually succeed in implicating my daughter in the UN plot.'

'Why are you telling me all of this?' I asked after a quick look past Nolan and down the block. Empty.

'Isn't this what bad guys do? Reveal the details of their sordid plans to the hero right before he saves the day?'

'Makes for a good movie, sure, but it rarely happens in real life.'

'Well then, how about I'm being candid because you deserve to know the truth. You are a good detective and against lesser minds, I have no doubt you would have prevailed. I respect you, which is why I haven't killed you. Besides, anything I've said cannot be proven. I possess the datapad. And the one piece of evidence you did have, you threw down an alley for some poor guy to find.' He glanced up at the sky. 'Now, if you'll excuse me, I must be going.'

Lesser minds, some guy.

'You're not getting away this time, Kitterman!' I drew the NEEDLE and fired in one fluid motion.

At that range, he couldn't react fast enough to completely avoid the projectile and the dart buried itself in his shoulder. The charge should incapacitate him in a matter of seconds. Time seemed to slow down and I watched expectantly. Nothing happened.

I had the wrong charge in the damn gun.

He laughed and plucked the dart out of his shoulder, tossing it on the ground. 'Your lack of attention to detail, Mr Helmqvist. It is what will cost you success in your endeavours.'

Every muscle in my body tensed in anticipation of Kitterman reneging on his decision to kill me, but it never happened. Instead, Ashdown came screeching around the corner.

Kitterman picked up his satchel and began running east. I stood there, bewildered, watching him go.

'Get in the damn car!' Ashdown had opened the passenger side door and yelled through it. I tucked the NEEDLE into the waist of jeans at the small of my back and sprinted towards the detective.

We lost Kitterman when he rounded a corner, but it didn't matter. We knew his destination: a large industrial complex adjacent to the edge of the IM's dome called The New London Excavation and Salvage Company.

They specialised in mining raw materials from a quarry located on the eastern perimeter of the *Chryse Planitia*. The company also recovered spent water silos from the hydration delivery field, located to the south-east of the IM, and recycled them for use in other industries.

NLESC was one of the few non-governmental operations outside the Spaceport with permission for an airlock. It must have been how he entered the city without being detected. If he made it to the exit before we could catch him, that would be it. He'd escape with the evidence.

We raced through the empty streets of the IM dome. The dashboard strobe light flickered blue. A siren, tucked somewhere in the engine compartment, wailed.

'Call Metro Dispatch access code three-zero-three!' Ashdown shouted to no one. The ringing of a phone replaced the cries of the siren.

'Metro Dispatch.'

'Metro, this is Detective Ashdown. Badge number two-five-one-seven. I am in chase of a person of interest, heading east towards New London Excavation and Salvage. I believe his intent is to breach the airlock at the facility and escape onto the surface. Send interior and exterior units forthwith. Please have the outside unit bring two additional Pursuit EVA suits.' He glanced over at me. 'Both size large. Subject may not be armed but is extremely dangerous.' I nodded my agreement.

'Roger that 2517. Units are being mobilised now.'

'Thank you Dispatch. Ashdown out.'

The call terminated and the sirens resumed their screeching.

About 30 seconds later, we closed in on Kitterman as he neared a service door in one of the high metal walls that ringed in the piles of junk in NLESC's scrap yard. Ashdown jammed on the brakes and brought the vehicle to a sudden stop. The detective was out of his seat. Before I had a chance to undo my seatbelt, he drew a model of pistol I'd never seen before and aimed it over the doorframe in Kitterman's direction.

'Metro Police! Don't move!' he barked. Naturally, Kitterman moved. He kicked the door through and completely off its hinges like some sort of cheap movie prop. Ashdown squeezed off two rounds. Lances of blue light about 15 centimetres long streaked towards Nolan. He slipped through the doorway. The shots went wide of the mark anyway and energy dissipated along the wall.

I had at long last extracted myself from the car and watched with fascination. 'What are you using?' I asked as I glanced at the weapon from over the car roof.

Ashdown started to move. I followed. 'It's new. An Enfield PEP mark one.' He had it low to his side and we reached the wall with caution.

'Pep?' I asked when we reached the outer wall.

'Pulsed Energy Pistol. The weapon fires a non-lethal electrical bolt. The clip holds a battery with enough juice for twelve shots. It's effective against humans and androids alike... Look, Helm, can we talk about this later? Maybe when we aren't chasing someone?'

'Yeah. Sorry. After you.'

Ashdown spun and squared up to the doorway in a modified Weaver stance. Once he cleared the doorway, I slipped in behind him.

Between us and a cube of a building that ran right up to the dome sat huge piles of twisted metal and remnants of giant capsule-shaped water containers. Kitterman was nowhere in sight. Ashdown swept from side to side as he advanced towards an entrance door at a careful pace. With so many hiding spots and blind turns, our quarry had the advantage.

As we cleared a couple of huge mounds of junk, I caught the flash of metal out of the corner of my eye from left and behind us. Ash-down didn't see it. I rolled out of the way. Ashdown took it like he was a change-up left up in the zone. The blow from the large, thin-walled section of aluminium ductwork sent him face down in the dirt. A groan told me the detective wasn't dead. A pile of scrap swallowed up his gun.

I charged Kitterman. At about 2 metres distance, I leapt. Left hand leading the way, right hand cocked back to deliver a haymaker from an elevated position. Kitterman hopped back. I landed. He dipped under my attack and countered with a palm strike to my chest. The blow sent me backwards. I landed on my ass, gasping for breath.

Nolan looked up from me towards the sound of more sirens. He left me on the ground and ran for the door of the building. I rolled Ashdown over and checked on him. He was already starting to stir.

Tough as nails, that one.

I clutched my chest and chased after Kitterman. Before I reached the doorway, I tossed my NEEDLE deep into a giant pile of twisted metal. I didn't see the point in carrying an obviously antiquated piece of weaponry anymore and its discovery on my person would only get me in trouble.

The airlock consisted of a massive 3-door system in a 12-metre diameter, 50-metre-long shaft. Standard protocol dictated that two of the three doors had to be engaged at all times. Any sort of failure of one of the locks could be catastrophic. Most facilities had all three closed when not in use. One can never be too careful.

Locks of the size used by NLESC also came with service hatches next to the airlock to allow workers in and out of the tunnel without having to burn a lot of energy on opening the giant portals. The exception was the airlock that led directly to the Martian surface. It didn't have a service hatch.

Kitterman had bypassed the access doors' security features by rip-ping them off their hinges. When I made it to the first lock, I found the hatch at my feet.

A straight shot through the middle hatch, I saw Nolan working at a furious pace to override the exterior lock. I had only made it into the first chamber, when he glanced over his shoulder and spotted me. The disk holding the harsh Martian environment at bay began to open.

'Give it up, Mr Helmqvist,' Nolan Kitterman shouted. Air began escaping past me and into the thinner atmosphere. 'Where I go, you cannot follow.'

I had no way of knowing the position of the exterior police unit. I had to hope that they were close.

The pull of the world beyond the dome increased as the crack widened. I gripped the doorframe of the second access hatch with every ounce of strength I had left.

'This isn't over, Kitterman!' A hollow threat perhaps, but I had to say something. He responded by laughing again.

'Once again, your lack of attention to detail, Mr Helmqvist. You have been outwitted at every turn. And now, I bid you adieu,' he said with a slight bow.

When the door had opened about halfway, Kitterman leapt past it and vanished into the night.

I let go of the one thing keeping me inside and skidded along the ground towards the exit. I hit the partially exposed door so hard that it knocked the wind out of me. Pain coursed through my not-fully-healed body. I hadn't even noticed Ashdown. He'd slid along the wall next to me and pounded the emergency close button.

Moments later, the door made a resounding bang. The air pressure normalised and breathing came easier with each gasp. Ashdown offered a hand and pulled me to my feet.

'Metro Dispatch access code three-zero-three,' he called into his earpiece.

'Metro Dispatch. Go ahead.'

'This is Ashdown. Where the hell are my Speeders?'

'There are two units en route to your position. ETA three minutes.'

'Dammit! The suspect is outside. We'll lose him if they don't hurry.'

'Should I have them pursue two-five-one-seven?'

CHAPTER TWENTY-SIX

'No! Just tell them to get their asses here!'

'Roger that.'

A lot can happen in three minutes, it seems. In that span of time, two squad cars arrived on the scene and Ashdown had them combing the salvage yard. In the airlock, we had donned temporary breathing masks we'd found in an emergency supply cabinet. Ashdown and I lashed ourselves to the airlock wall and he reopened the exterior portal.

When the Speeders arrived, he closed the lock only long enough for us to squirm into a light-weight version of the standard issue EVA suit. They offered adequate protection from the elements; however, the smaller respirator unit attached under the helmet's chin provided only one hour's worth of oxygen. They called them Pursuit EVAs because you could get them on quickly. By the time we were outside the airlock, discussing our next move, we had given Nolan Kitterman at least a five-minute head start.

For a guy who could move as fast as he could, it might as well have been 30 minutes.

27

'Did you see anyone out here?' barked Ashdown to the lead officer.

'Umm. No, sir.'

I found a set of prints. 'His tracks head east.'

'We came from the south,' the officer interjected as reason for them not seeing a man running across a landscape not conducive to hosting marathons.

'We don't have a lot of time. Helmqvist and I will ride with you,' he said to the lead officer.

Outside the airlock floated two hovercrafts. They seated four, were open-topped and bore a striking resemblance to a similar vehicle found on a fictional desert planet in a distant galaxy. I didn't know their actual name, but everyone knew them as 'Speeders'.

Ashdown and I took the rear seats as the lead Speeder pilot and his partner took the front. When the other team were ready, the officer gunned it. I gripped a bar mounted in front of me for fear of flying out of the cabin.

The vehicles glided over the rough Martian terrain with ease. Kitterman's tracks arced from due east to south in the direction of a cluster of large, white water silos jutting out of the ground like a mouthful of broken teeth from rust-coloured gums. When we were about 800 metres from the water field, the area lit up with the intense glow of an engine firing. By the time we reached the silos, a personal spacecraft rocketed towards the heavens.

Our pilot brought the Speeder to a halt and we all stared up at the night's sky, watching the ship until it vanished from sight.

'What would you like to do, Detective?' the pilot asked.

'Call in the launch and then let's investigate the Water Field.'

The area known as the Water Field earned its name because it is where New London receives its supply of water from Titan. A company on that moon harvests ice and sells it to colonies within the solar system that do not have their own source of H2O. What water existed on Mars had been used up long ago.

The company packs large, cylindrical containers with frozen liquid, and transports them from Titan with the equivalent of an interplanetary lorry with space fold capabilities. When the delivery vehicle reaches a planet like Mars, it enters a low orbit and launches the containers to a drop zone on the surface of the planet. A combination of homing beacons in our water field, and proximity sensors on the container, guide it in a controlled descent to an open spot in the field.

Once they touch down, legs extend to support the silo. A solar panel array powers a heating element to melt the ice and keeps the temperature at a steady 10 degrees Celsius. Eventually, New London Water and Power send out a convoy of collection tankers to drain the silo. These trucks deliver the precious water to a processing plant located in the Spaceport. New London Salvage retrieve the abandoned silos, recycle them, and sell them to factories within the city.

The system might have seemed overly complicated but it worked. And since the delivery vehicles didn't have to expend a ton of energy to land every time they brought a fresh supply of water, it kept the costs down and water from becoming a luxury item.

The pilot did as instructed, and then accelerated the Speeder to a slow crawl. Kitterman's trail led us through a maze of the large, ashen silos that had not yet been drained or salvaged. At the far edge of the field, we found a storage tower unlike the others in size and overall shape. The footprints went straight to it.

In the far distance, a swirling mass of dust and rock rumbled towards us. Traces of lightning coursed through the chaos of dirt and wind. In the dark, it was quite dramatic.

'A storm is coming, Helm. We have to make this quick.'

He and I jumped out of the craft before we had come to a complete stop and immediately scanned the silo. The sides had been split open wide like space shuttle bay doors and the top of the tower was flipped back like the cap on a tube of toothpaste. Inside there looked to be some sort of launch platform. A layer of soot, charred metal and a ruined control panel were all that remained.

'This is new,' John said to no one in particular over his comm. unit.

It wasn't a question, but I chimed in just the same. 'What do you mean?'

'I've not seen, or heard of, anyone using a storage tank to hide a launch pad in. The captain needs to know about this. It might help explain smuggling operations into the city.'

I walked around the unit to see if there were any other clues that might help us. A flight plan fixed to one of the walls would have been extremely helpful.

'Can you get a forensic team out here?' I asked.

'Maybe in the morning.' He glanced up again. 'But the tempest coming might ruin any evidence to be found.'

Our pilot broke in over the airwaves. 'Dispatch has notified us that the approaching dust storm is a class three. We have to get a move on, Detective.'

Dust storms on Mars are dangerous for reasons that aren't immediately obvious. For all their menace, winds topping 200 km/h and particles of Martian topsoil caught in those winds aren't the threat. On a planet without a real atmosphere, and a gravity the fraction of Earth's outside New London, the force isn't even enough to knock a person down, or cause a tear in the skin of their EVA. The real danger is the static electricity created by fine particles of dirt colliding into each other. Surges of lightning will kill electronics. Short out life support systems. Kill you slowly. Unless you get hit by too many bolts. Then you die pretty quickly. Either way, all of us were looking at a bad ending if we didn't get going.

'Fine. Let's go,' he announced.

The wind had begun to pick up. Particles of dust and small debris swirled around us and pelted us. If we weren't encased in suits designed to keep us alive, I have no doubt I could've felt the charge in the air. But I didn't have to feel it to know. The HUD in my visor began to flicker.

We scrambled back into the speeder and our pilot gunned it. The other craft already started for home ahead of us. Our man guided the craft through the field. When we cleared the last silo, I glanced back to see a twisting, churning mass of Martian landscape tumbling towards us.

The Speeder pilot opened up the throttle and we began to out-pace it. Our tiny craft created its own wake of red dirt as he pushed it to the very limit of its speed. As we neared the substation airlock, I could see it was already open. The lead craft entered and made a hard left to clear the area.

'Bravo 923.' That was us. 'You are coming in too fast. Be advised you will hit the interior lock door at this speed. Do you copy?'

No one said anything. All four of us poured our will into out-stripping the hurricane.

I glanced back. The cloud looked like gods fighting. Brilliant bursts of white blinked here and there, reflecting off the visor of my EVA. The sheer power of it held me in temporary awe.

It gained energy. The distance between the maelstrom and us narrowed. We could not go fast enough. Bolts of energy arced out of the cloud like some nightmare forged in the mind of Tesla. Systems on the craft began to flicker. I only hoped they didn't begin to fail. Once again, I latched onto the bar in front of me with a vice-like grip.

'Bravo 9… I repea… ou… opy?'

'Yeah, I copy! Now shut the hell up! Everyone, brace for impact!'

Tendrils of electricity grabbed the Speeder and all hell broke loose in our tiny little world. Display panels popped, and smoked, and went dead. In one last hurrah, the engines spat a gout of fire and then nothing.

We hit the ground hard and skipped over a dune. It nearly kicked me out of my seat. The Speeder slid through the sand, rocks and gravel, sparks all around us, but the pilot had positioned it perfectly. It bounced through the external airlock and came to a stop about 2 metres before the second airlock door. Its counterpart slammed closed with a resounding thud. Before I had the time to process everything, let alone relax my grip on the bar, the tumbling mass of Martian topsoil and coursing energy unleashed itself on the wall of the dome. However, the dust and the wind and the electricity could not penetrate the engineering marvel that is New London's domes.

The inner door opened. A tech group ran into the hanger and doused the still smouldering engines with fire suppressing foam. I didn't dare move. It felt like hours before the pilot broke silence. 'Helluva a ride, eh boys?'

The co-pilot busted out laughing.

These guys weren't right in the head.

By the time I had given Ashdown a statement outlining my activity up to the moment I called him, hopped a subway back to RD1 to fetch my car, drove home, hid my FE9 in the closet, and drank myself stupid, I hadn't been passed out for very long. A persistent chirp from my MAX smartwatch pulled me from a deep, dreamless sleep.

Less than half awake, my hand knocked into an empty lowball glass and bourbon bottle reaching for it. I checked the display. Ashdown.

'Detective, to what do I owe the pleasure?'

'Helmqvist, is that you?'

'You dialled my number! Who else would it be?' Pain in my chest sent me into a coughing fit. I tried to cover the mic as best as possible.

'Sorry, I didn't recognise your voice at first. You sound like shit.'

'Your people skills haven't improved much, Ash. Again, why are you calling me?'

'I briefed my LT on last night's incident and he wanted to speak with you. You down for another visit to our lovely precinct?' He pronounced LT: *el-tee*.

I was lying on the couch and rubbed the spot where Kitterman had punched me the night before. 'Sure, why not,' I said at last.

'Great! I'll pick you up in thirty.'

He hung up before I had a chance to propose a time much later in the day.

In light of how badly things had gone with the Kitterman case, I decided to lay out all my cards for the police. Well maybe not all of them, but enough of them to maybe convince Ashdown's boss of what'd been going on at MARA Corporation.

Thirty minutes gave me just enough time to shower and dump the video images from last night onto my MIX12. A quick survey of what I had didn't fill me with confidence. Kitterman's flat cap obscured most of the photos. I couldn't use any of the CCTV footage for obvious reasons. Ashdown may have gotten a look at him, but if that helped, I didn't know.

If you had Nolan sitting in an interview room, or better yet a courtroom, you might be able to make a convincing argument. But with him cruising around space, and even with Ashdown's account, I doubt anyone would believe he had returned from the grave. Trying to get his lieutenant to buy it may have been a fool's errand, but I had to try.

I waited outside for Ashdown to show. He stopped in front of me and opened the passenger door. Immediately, I was hit with the smell of coffee. A bag of doughnuts all but waved hello to me from the passenger seat. I grabbed the doughnuts and took their place. A cup of Joe steamed away in a holder.

'Based on the way you sounded over the phone, I thought you might need these.'

'If I had any friends, Ash, I'd put you right near the top.'

The detective hammered the accelerator and we raced off in the general direction of RD1. 'That's a big if, Helm. You aren't the most likeable person I've ever met.'

'Pot calling the kettle black,' I replied with a mouthful of dough-nut.

'Shut up and eat.'

We drove in silence while I ate. When I'd finished we were close to Metro HQ.

Chapter Twenty-Seven

'Do you think your boss'll believe what happened?'

'You mean Nolan Kitterman returns from the dead, pays a visit to his daughter, and you chase him through the streets of New London?'

'Something like that, yeah.'

'Depends on what else you've got.'

I glanced down at the MIX12. 'A few things.'

We stopped outside the main entrance in an area marked 'Police Vehicles Only'. A few minutes later, Ashdown knocked on the doorframe of his superior's office. The door was open but Ashdown knocked anyway.

'Detective Ashdown, please come in.' The lieutenant didn't look up from a MIX11. We sat in the two chairs opposite his desk.

When he'd finished whatever it was he was doing he looked up and smiled.

'Daniel Helmqvist is it?'

'That's right.'

'Lieutenant Stone, but everyone calls me Wave.' He leaned across the desk to shake hands. I leaned in as well and met him halfway.

'Nice to meet you, lieutenant.'

I'd put him in his early fifties. His short, wavy, auburn hair came with a pair of matching sideburns and a thick moustache. He looked like he'd travelled through time to our century from the Age of Disco and decided he liked it too much here to leave.

Lieutenant Stone rocked back in his chair. 'I have read Detective Ashdown's report concerning last night's activities, but I have a few questions you might be able to clear up for me.'

'What would you like to know?'

'Can you take me through your steps prior to contacting Detective Ashdown?'

He only meant that night. I knew that. However, like I said, I decided to tell them more. My client was alive – in so far as a machine is alive – but I didn't really have a case anymore. Or so I thought. Therefore, in as vague terms as possible, I laid it all out there. I didn't mention my client, my illegal activities or what was really on the datapad. I spun it as a recovery of stolen property.

When I finished the tale, he looked at me and reflected on what he had heard. At last, all he said was what I'd already heard, 'Nolan Kitterman is dead.'

Ashdown chimed in to my aid. 'With all due respect, sir, the suspect we pursued last night bore a striking resemblance to Nolan Kitterman.'

'Why did you leave that out of your report?'

John flushed a bit. 'I didn't think you'd take it seriously. That you'd think it was some sort of joke.'

Lieutenant Stone's gaze bounced from Ashdown to myself and back to him. He had a very easy manner about him. 'You're right. I would have taken it to be some sort of typo, or possibly even a joke. The man is dead.'

I pulled out my MIX12. 'Lieutenant, if you can enable your MIX's Cargo Drop feature to Everyone, I can swipe a video to your tablet.'

He jabbed the touchscreen on his tablet a few times. Lieutenant Dave Stone appeared in my list of available Cargo Drop users. When I saw his first name, his nickname, Wave, made a bit more sense. I selected his name, grabbed the video feed from last night with my index finger and digitally flicked it towards his machine.

He sent the video to a smart-glass screen on his wall to allow all three of us to watch it plus a slide show of zoomed-in still shots I had added because you never know what might help and what might not. I provided commentary.

'A very unusual angle, Mr Helmqvist.'

'Call me Dan.'

'Okay. Were they through a skylight?'

Crimson patches grew on my cheeks. 'Umm… yeah. It was a stakeout.' I couldn't let this turn into a conversation about me trespassing so I continued. 'But right here…' I hopped out of my seat and began pointing at still images. 'That's Mara Kitterman. And this is Nolan Kitterman.'

'I can see that that is Mara but I'm not buying that that other person is Nolan. I just don't see it.'

Ashdown added his two cents. 'His clothing matches the guy we chased into the salvage yard.'

'Do you think this is Nolan Kitterman, returned from the grave, Detective?'

Stone had put John in a tight spot. His next answer would either help me or hurt me. My gut told me, John would look out for his career before he tried to help a guy to whom he owed no loyalty.

'I dunno, Lieutenant. He fits the description of how Nolan Kitterman looks in all the media photos at the time of his death. But this guy was also fast and very strong. I believe he could have used lethal force last night but didn't. Does that all add up to Mara Kitterman's father pulling a Lazarus? I dunno. There is too much circumstantial evidence to say yes.'

I fell back into my chair in a slump. My only chance at getting some traction in my case had vanished like that rocket ship last night. In vain, I pressed on. 'At the very least, you can make a connection between the suspect and Mara Kitterman. The detective admitted they are the same person.'

'And?'

'And? And? He assaulted Detective Ashdown. Surely that is enough to question Kitterman's relationship with this man?!'

Stone looked back at Ashdown. Ashdown gave him an 'I'd rather not be involved with this' shrug.

The lieutenant redirected his attentions to me. 'All you've shown me is a video of a man whose features cannot be ID'd, obtained through suspicious means. I'm not going to go to one of the most influential people in this city with half-baked accusations of theft, and a dead guy who happens to be her father running through our streets, belting police officers with large pieces of scrap metal. I like my job, thank-you-very-much. I believe everyone in this precinct likes their job far too much to go down that path.'

The finality of Stone's verdict, the acknowledgement of how poorly I had conducted my investigation, the last words of Nolan Kitterman, all rang in my head like a church bell mourning the lost. I struggled against the anger welling up inside of me and stood to make my exit.

'Fine,' I choked out.

Ashdown and Lt Stone rose from their seats as well. Stone's polite demeanour never changed. Even though he had shut me down with practised skill, he never wavered from being polite. 'I appreciate you taking the time to chat with us, Dan. Detective Ashdown can show you out.'

You're welcome somehow escaped my lips before I could get out of his office.

We rode down in the elevator in silence. Neither Ashdown nor I had anything to say to each other. When we hit the ground floor, I stepped out. He did not.

'Stay outta trouble, Helm,' he said once more.

Instead of a witty retort, I kept going without looking back.

28

With Nolan Kitterman in the wind, a police department who didn't believe me and nothing to connect Mara to a terrorist attack on Earth, I had a couple of loose ends to tie up before I could close this case.

I grabbed a taxi from Metro HQ back to my place. Once there, I changed into a smart, heather-grey, wool-blend three-piece because appearances mattered. After that, I drove the LTI to Theo's for a trade in. The Griffon had been fixed a week ago, and I missed my baby. En route, I stopped for a couple of bacon and egg sandwiches and two cups of coffee from a nearby deli. This routine of bringing food was starting to feel like a ritual to some ancient pagan god. A sacrifice of foodstuffs required before he would agree to entreaty with me.

For Theo's part, he was delighted to see the sandwich and hot beverage. He assured me he had forgotten to eat before he came into work. We both laughed at the obvious lie and enjoyed the quick meal. On my way out, I settled my bill with him, which was far lower than it should have been for the repairs.

At that time of the morning, cars, buses and taxis reduced traffic flow to a crawl. It took me nearly three quarters of an hour to reach the main entrance of MARA Corp. A security guard stopped me at the gate and asked my business. I told him I was there to see Mara Kitterman and no, I didn't have an appointment. He stepped into his little booth, called it in, and then waved me through. To be perfectly honest, I wasn't sure I'd be allowed to set foot inside the building but there you go. I found an available parking space reserved for guests and brought the Griffon to a stop between the white lines.

A very large reception desk, placed exactly in the middle of the very impressive foyer of MARA Corporation, represented my next hurdle. I gave the receptionist my name. She made another phone call and I waited patiently. After she hung up, she gave me instructions on how to find Mara Kitterman's office. As if I didn't already know.

All of the activity on the floor made me feel a tad bit unsettled. It was so peaceful and quiet the last time. I looked around nervously and then set out for Kitterman's office. At a desk planted right outside Kitterman's door sat Charlotte Rennick. I stopped dead in my tracks and gaped at her like an idiot. Of all the things I didn't expect, Rennick at a desk working away like nothing had happened took the number one spot.

'Can I help you?' she asked. The girlish tone that she once possessed had vanished. Now she sounded more like her creator minus the accent.

'Um, yeah. I'm here to see Mara Kitterman.'

'Is she expecting you?'

'I believe so.'

'Your name?'

'Daniel Helmqvist.'

When she heard my name, I detected a noticeable change in her expression. I began to wonder if somewhere deep in the recesses of her memory the mention of my name sparked a hint of recognition. She picked up a phone and made a call to her boss. She never took her eyes off of me.

'You may go in,' she stated after she had hung up the phone.

I walked into Kitterman's office. Mara sat at the very desk I had used as a hiding spot from the not-quite-diligent security guard a lifetime ago. She stood as I entered.

'Please, take a seat, Mr Helmqvist,' she said, and pointed to one of the armchairs facing her desk. 'Would you like anything to drink?'

I sat in the proffered seat. 'No thanks. I'm not planning on staying for too long.'

'Very well, Mr Helmqvist. What brings you here, then?'

'I just wanted you to know that I know it was you.'

'Me? What do you mean?'

'New York City. Giant explosion. Most of the lower east side reduced to rubble. Any of that ring a bell?'

CHAPTER TWENTY-EIGHT

'Naturally, Mr Helmqvist. It was a horrible day.'

'Beyond words, Ms Kitterman, and I know you were responsible for it. I know you planned it and were instrumental in the execution of the bombing, which killed tens of thousands.'

She sat back down in her high-backed executive leather chair, arms crossed primly on her lap, and regarded me with her impassive, scientific eyes. Time passed into that uncomfortable area where it's just two people looking at each other. I have to admit, it made me uneasy. Her eyes narrowed, and then after a couple of seconds, her face lit up with the sudden realisation that I had nothing on her.

A Cheshire grin pulled at the corner of her lips.

'Even if I did do something as horrible as you suggest, Mr Helmqvist, you have no proof, do you? Because if you did, you would have been accompanied by a police escort.'

'Short of you volunteering a confession, you got me there, Mara. The proof, which I am certain does exist, flew off into the night. Secreted away into our vast galaxy by a ghost.'

'A ghost, you say?'

Her smile was impossibly wide and I could not help but notice how beautiful she looked – in a wild, dangerous sort of way.

'Can you set your Cargo Drop to Everyone?'

She did so.

I produced my MIX12 from a satchel and went through the same motions as I did with Lieutenant Stone. She hit play and a smart-glass display on her desk lit up. It replayed everything I had shown the police. Her smile faded as she watched.

'I could have you arrested for trespassing,' she said after tapping the stop button.

'Yeah, Metro hinted at the same thing.'

'You have shown this to the police?'

'Earlier today. I was summoned by a lieutenant to give an account of a run-in a detective and I had with your father last night.'

Her laughter was spontaneous and resonated throughout her office.

'My father? He has been dead for nearly twenty years. Science has not advanced *that* far. My father… You certainly have an active imagination, Mr Helmqvist.'

'Cut the theatrics, Mara. We both know it's Nolan Kitterman, or a copy of him. He told me as much last night.' Getting laughed at again started to rub me the wrong way. 'The only thing preventing you from spending the rest of your life in the joint is that he managed to escape. You got lucky, Kitterman, and that's all there is to it.'

'Say what you will, Mr Helmqvist, but what matters most is what you can prove and what you cannot prove. And, from the looks of it, you cannot prove very much at all. If you will excuse me, there are more important matters that require my attention.'

'Perhaps you'll indulge me one more question before I go?'

'Is it as ridiculous as the rest?'

'You'll probably think so.'

'Alright, ask your question.'

'It might have a follow-up question or two.'

'Now you are trying my patience!'

'Does MARA Corp own a private hangar and dock in the Spaceport?'

'Naturally. As do many other businesses in this city.'

'That explains a lot then.'

'Explains what, exactly?'

'How Nolan came and went unnoticed. I'm guessing the ship out in the Water Field was an emergency-only kind of thing.'

She affected another sigh. 'Yes, it was as ridiculous as the others. I think we are done here, Mr Helmqvist.'

She turned her attention to her computer monitor. I stood up and fired one last parting shot.

'What you said earlier: you're right, Mara. I can't prove a whole hell of a lot, but, like I said, I know. I know what you did and what kind of person you are. You're a killer and a sociopath and you stink of evil.'

With that, I turned and started to walk out before she had a chance at a response. I heard her call for security and told her not to bother. My work here was done. She did bother, though. A couple of hard boys roughly the same cut as the ones I shared a ride with in Kitterman's limo met me at the elevators and unceremoniously escorted me to the main entrance.

On the way out, I passed Rennick once again. She wore that look we all do when we're trying to connect a face to a memory.

Later that day, something must have clicked because she showed up at my office. I was busy typing up some notes on the case, you know for posterity and all that crap, when I saw none other than Charlotte Rennick standing in my doorway. I briefly wondered why Pam hadn't announced her presence. Pam probably had her reasons.

I motioned to one of the two tired armchairs across from my desk. 'Ms Rennick, please take a seat.'

She sat down in that same prim and proper manner as her creator and we locked gazes for a moment. Those viridian pools were still something I could fall into and drown. I cleared my throat and blinked a few times to ward off her emerald spell.

'What can I do for you today?'

'Your assistant confirmed that I had hired you to locate something,' she asked without the inflection.

I decided to roll the dice and proceeded to tell her the entire story of how we met and that she had hired me to find a storage device. Unlike at the police station, I told it to her straight. She asked questions along the way and eventually we arrived at today. I had a few questions of my own and she answered them to the best of her ability. It seemed as if I was partially right about the extent of her memory wipe. However, when she saw me today, it sparked a host of recollections. 'What I can't fathom, Charlotte, is how you didn't know you were an android?' I asked in the silence that had settled in the room.

She sat in contemplation. 'Are you familiar with Emergent Behaviour and its applications in artificial intelligence?'

I glanced past Rennick to where Pam was sitting. 'Machines that learn. They adapt their reasoning for problem solving. The goal is to make them more intuitive. That still doesn't answer my question about why you thought you were a human.'

Her gaze dropped down to her lap where her hands rested. 'What does it mean to be human? To be a biological organism? Flesh and bone as it were?'

She certainly looked flesh and bone. 'That's part of it. Maybe not all of it. Love. Hate. Emotions. Experiences. Free thought. Self-awareness on an abstract level, I guess.'

Charlotte looked back up at me. 'What if an organism possessed all of those things but was not biological? What if advances in Emergent Behaviour could revolutionise the way a machine viewed the world around them? That they could transcend problem-solving and actually reason. Would they be considered human?'

'For the most part, sure,' I answered. 'But I doubt a human would ever accept them on equal terms. We see the world, and judge it, according to the experiences that made us who we are. Skin colour. Language. Political beliefs. Religious beliefs. Sexual orientation. Climate. Height. Weight. You name it and we use it to define ourselves, and to marginalise the Other. We take great delight in finding differences. A lot of human life has been wasted in this pursuit.'

'I see.' She paused again before continuing. 'Mara Kitterman has confessed to me that Transilience began as an attempt to bring her father back from the dead. Between her work in Emergent Behaviour and advances in synthesising the neural transmission network of the human brain, she devised a means in which to transfer consciousness. Nolan Kitterman was created from a combination of Mara's own recollections, and a holographic programme he had left her.'

My showdown with Nolan flashed through my memory. 'Yeah, he mentioned the programme the other night right before he escaped out an airlock.'

'He became her proof of concept.'

'No kidding. He seems to possess the best of both worlds. He obviously cares a great deal for Mara – as a father should – but he takes full advantage of the fact that he is an android.'

'With the success of Nolan Kitterman,' Charlotte continued as if I hadn't said anything, 'Mara created three more units. One was sent to Earth. The other two are here on Mars.'

'Nolan told me the fourth unit was the one that destroyed the UN,' I interrupted.

'Based on what Mara has inferred since my report, that makes sense. Another was James. And then there was me. Who James is modelled after, or why he behaved the way that he did, is unknown to me. Mara has not repaired him and she will not tell me anything about him.'

'I can tell you what little I know. He seemed to know he was a synthetic. When my rifle shot put him in a junk pile, he shouldn't have been able to get up. But he acted like nothing happened. I can also tell you he's nuts and he should be scrapped for parts.'

Charlotte waited longer than it was comfortable before responding. I started to regret my comments. Even if they were true.

'I served as her grand experiment. A means to build upon all her research and scientific discovery that went into creating Nolan, as well as a means to understand acceptance. Could an android ever be perceived as equal to a human? That is the question she set out to answer when she created me.'

'It's pretty ironic that she's concerned with acceptance on any level given her prejudices against... ah, what was the phrase again... oh yeah... the lesser races, which have infected the great epicentres of civilisation.'

She nodded again. 'It is illogical.'

I waited for more but nothing came.

Fortunately, Rennick rescued the conversation. 'We were discussing my not knowing I was an android. Should we continue with that?'

'Yes, please.'

'Mara allowed me to function autonomously. I had an apartment. A very good career. A bank account. An annual pass for the Underground. An ordinary life by Martian standards. She also instilled an intense work ethic with very little interest in social life outside MARA Corporation as an attempt to minimise the risk of my true nature being discovered. I had no idea I was anything but a living, breathing human female.'

'If someone else found out you were an android, then you would know you're an android and her experiment would be compromised, right?'

'Something like that, yes.'

'And yet, a couple of weeks ago, you paid me a visit at the 3rd Street. I'm guessing you began to function a little too autonomously?'

'Yes. I believe Mara underestimated the level of self-awareness capable within a machine. She did not count on the possibility that I might become independent in thought and action. I think she also underestimated the side effects of installing that datapad inside me. Although I did not have direct access to the information contained on it, echoes of the data drifted into my consciousness. It's how I knew she was responsible for the New York bombing without actually knowing; if that makes any sense.'

'Not really, but then again most of this is hard to believe.'

'May I ask you something?'

'Sure. Go for it.'

'Did you know I was not a human?'

I shook my head. 'Not a clue. Not until I found you at the abandoned bottling factory. Maybe if I had tried to get to know you… umm… intimately, I would have learned the truth.'

Her cheeks flushed a pale crimson. The level of detail. I couldn't believe it. A machine that could blush. Maybe I wouldn't have known even if we had gotten intimate.

'What is your first memory?' I asked.

'Waking up one Monday morning and getting ready for work. I had a dream of a large estate with a fountain at the centre of a lovely garden. I sat on a stone bench reading a book.' She paused for a moment. 'I assume it was one of Mara's memories, but I still find it pleasant to reflect on that day and that dream.'

'And that was it? Just an average person from then on?'

'I had no reason to suspect otherwise. I am in perfect health. Never been sick. Never been injured. No reason to visit anyone who might tell me I'm not an actual human being. I've never been close enough to someone who might have reason to suspect I was anything but a living, breathing person.'

I rubbed my forehead with my fingertips and dragged them down my face past my chin. My hands dropped onto my desk with a quiet thud.

'I guess that answers the question.'

'How I didn't know I was an android?'

'Yep. And we know why you are here: to answer some questions you had.'

She nodded.

'Does Mara know you're here?'

She paused before answering. An expression of concentration washed over her face, like she was trying to remember something. 'Real time data indicates that she does not. She believes I am in Research District 2.'

'What? How?'

'Because I have manipulated her monitoring system into believing that that is my current location.'

'Unbelievable. It's only been a few days since you've come back online and you're already sneaking out of the office.'

'I had to know the rest of the story. I needed to know how this ended. Plus, she did not, or could not, fundamentally change who I am. I am her and she is me. We have our differences but we are essentially the same person.'

'But she killed thousands of people. You don't strike me as someone capable of murder.'

'I'll take that as a compliment. As I said, we have our differences. Perhaps I represent an aspect of her that is more innocent. A Mara Kitterman that has not been infected by the vitriol of a father who tried to assign meaning to a random act of violence.'

I drummed my fingers on the desk, trying to make sense of all this.

'Also, I have a debt to settle for services rendered. If I recall correctly, we agreed to five hundred a day plus expenses. Is eight thousand credits acceptable?'

'I didn't get the evidence that you asked me to get. I failed. Eight grand is eight thousand more than I deserve on a job I thoroughly botched up.'

'Well, it is too late. I asked you out of social politeness,' she answered with a slight shrug of her shoulders. 'I have already paid your assistant, Pam, based on how long she said you have been working on my behalf.'

'Still, I am sorry that I wasn't able to retrieve the evidence, but thanks for the credits.'

Charlotte stood to turn and leave.

'So what's next?' I asked.

'I go back to work. Because I now know my true nature, Mara's experiment is effectively over. Nevertheless, it is where I belong.'

'So that's it? You're done with trying to expose her for the killer that she is?'

She glanced back at me through the doorway into my office as she crossed the space between Pam's desk and the exit. 'It is my sincere hope that someday justice will be served. Perhaps someone will find the means to do so,' she said as she backed out of my office and out of my life with a slight wave.

Pam swivelled around in her chair towards me but said nothing. My eyes shifted to my assistant, and I tried to glean meaning from her stoic expression. All of her quirks and mannerisms came into sharper focus. 'I'm sure you heard our entire conversation. What do you think, Pam? Has Emergent Behaviour transcended more than just problem solving? Are androids capable of emotions? Do their memories, and experiences, make them human? Should I be paying you a salary?' I cracked a wide grin on that last question.

She shook her head slowly, closed her eyes, turned back to her desk and began typing away at her usual furious pace. A few seconds later, she stopped and called out without looking at me. 'I do not require a salary. I am well provided for in this office.'

Her response carried too many questions for me to care about at the moment. 'Close out the case.'

'Yes, sir.'

I checked my MAX. Nearly 3pm. Happy hour somewhere in this damn galaxy. Good thing I had a mini bar in the desk drawer next to me. With a gin and tonic in hand, I rocked back in my worn-out executive and scrolled through my contact list.

'Why hello stranger,' Erica answered. I could almost hear the smile behind that song of a voice.

'Why hello yourself. Any plans for tonight?' I asked.

'Not at the moment.' Anticipation hung in the air.

'You up for a drink at the 3rd Street? Say around 8pm? I can introduce you to my favourite watering hole, and Curtis, the man who mixes the best drinks in the entire system.'

'Sure! That sounds perfect.'

'I'll pick you up at 7.30?'

'Great. See you then, Danny.'

'Looking forward to it.'

Acknowledgements

This novel began its life as a short story assignment in a creative writing course. Through a lot of blood, sweat and many tears, it germinated and grew into a tale that I am incredibly proud of. However, it could not have happened without the help of many amazing people.

I'd like to thank Scott Pack for giving my submission serious consideration. It had to be the most unusual submission I had ever made, and I still can't believe he helped make this happen. I'd also like to thank Xander for his patience and guidance through the funding campaign and production of *Transilience*. To the editorial staff at Unbound, I am deeply indebted to you. Annabel, Molly, Michael and everyone else who has worked on *Transilience*, you took what I thought was a pretty good story and made it great. Honestly, thank you. A thousand times thank you. I would also like to thank Mark and his talented staff in the art department for their incredible work on the cover design.

A warm thank you to several amazing people at Scribophile. You helped make me a better writer, and you know who you are. Also, a hearty thank you to my friend, Tom, who was kind enough to read several drafts of *Transilience*. Your advice on all things scientific was invaluable. And for everyone who has supported *Transilience* – thank you! Without your generosity, this novel would have never been realised. You are all amazing!

Finally, I cannot close this out without saying thank you to Jenny. Without your encouragement, your kindness and your understanding, I could not have written this. You are my greatest source of inspiration, my fiercest critic, and my biggest support. I am a better man with you in my life. Thank you.

Patrons List

Ali Burns
Steve Deppe
Mike Donald
Joseph Howley
Christopher Huang
Johari Ismail
Tim Merchant
Jeremy Thomas
Caleb Voronwë
Mark Walker
Eric Williams